P

Patricia Grace wa
of Ngati Raukawa
and is affiliated to Ngati Porou by marriage. She has
taught in primary and secondary schools in the King
Country, Northland and Porirua, where she now lives.
She is married with seven children.

Patricia Grace's stories have been published in a
number of periodicals and anthologies. Her first collection of stories, *Waiariki*, was published in 1975 (the first
collection of stories by a Maori woman writer), and a
second collection, *The Dream Sleepers*, in 1980. Her first
novel, *Mutuwhenua, The Moon Sleeps*, was published in
1978. She has also written two children's books in
English and Maori, illustrated by Robyn Kahukiwa, *The
Kuia and the Spider* (1981) and *Watercress Tuna and the
Children of Champion Street* (1985), the former winning
the Children's Picture Book of the Year award in 1982.
She also wrote the text for *Wahine Toa* (1984), illustrated
by Robyn Kahukiwa.

In 1985 Patricia Grace was the Writing Fellow at
Victoria University of Wellington.

Patricia Grace

WAIARIKI

PENGUIN BOOKS

Penguin Books (N.Z.) Ltd, 182–190 Wairau Road,
Auckland 10, New Zealand
Penguin Books Ltd, Harmondsworth,
Middlesex, England
Penguin Books; 40 West 23rd Street,
New York, N.Y.10010, U.S.A.
Penguin Books Australia Ltd, Ringwood,
Victoria, Australia
Penguin Books Canada Limited, 2801 John Street,
Markham, Ontario, Canada L3R 1B4

First published by Longman Paul Ltd 1975
Reprinted 1976, 1978, 1983
Published in Penguin Books 1986

Copyright © Patricia Grace 1975

Printed in Hong Kong

CONTENTS

ACKNOWLEDGEMENTS

Acknowledgements are due to the editors of *Landfall*, the *New Zealand Listener*, and *Te Ao Hou*, in which several of the stories in this book first appeared.

mo aku tamariki

A WAY OF TALKING

Rose came back yesterday; we went down to the bus to meet her. She's just the same as ever Rose. Talks all the time flat out and makes us laugh with her way of talking. On the way home we kept saying, 'E Rohe, you're just the same as ever.' It's good having my sister back and knowing she hasn't changed. Rose is the hard-case one in the family, the kama-kama one, and the one with the brains.

Last night we stayed up talking till all hours, even Dad and Nanny who usually go to bed after tea. Rose made us laugh telling about the people she knows, and taking off professor this and professor that from varsity. Nanny, Mum, and I had tears running down from laughing; e ta Rose we laugh-ed all night.

At last Nanny got out of her chair and said, 'Time for sleeping. The mouths steal the time of the eyes.' That's the lovely way she has of talking, Nanny, when she speaks in English. So we went to bed and Rose and I kept our mouths going for another hour or so before falling asleep.

This morning I said to Rose that we'd better go and get her measured for the dress up at Mrs Frazer's. Rose wanted to wait a day or two but I reminded her the wedding was only two weeks away and that Mrs Frazer had three frocks to finish.

'Who's Mrs Frazer anyway,' she asked. Then I remember-ed Rose hadn't met these neighbours though they'd been in the district a few years. Rose had been away at school.

'She's a dressmaker,' I looked for words. 'She's nice.'

'What sort of nice?' asked Rose.

'Rose, don't you say anything funny when we go up there,' I said. I know Rose, she's smart. 'Don't you get smart.' I'm older than Rose but she's the one that speaks out when something doesn't please her. Mum used to say, Rohe you've got the brains but you look to your sister for the sense. I started to feel funny about taking Rose up to Jane Frazer's because Jane often says the wrong thing without knowing.

We got our work done, had a bath and changed, and when Dad came back from the shed we took the station-wagon to drive over to Jane's. Before we left we called out to Mum, 'Don't forget to make us a Maori bread for when we get back.'

'What's wrong with your own hands,' Mum said, but she was only joking. Always when one of us comes home one of the first things she does is make a big Maori bread.

Rose made a good impression with her kamakama ways, and Jane's two nuisance kids took a liking to her straight away. They kept jumping up and down on the sofa to get Rose's attention and I kept thinking what a waste of a good sofa it was, what a waste of a good house for those two nuisance things. I hope when I have kids they won't be so hoha.

I was pleased about Jane and Rose. Jane was asking Rose all sorts of questions about her life in Auckland. About varsity and did Rose join in the marches and demonstrations. Then they went on to talking about fashions and social life in the city, and Jane seemed deeply interested. Almost as though she was jealous of Rose and the way she lived, as though she felt Rose had something better than a lovely house and clothes and everything she needed to make life good for her. I was pleased to see that Jane liked my sister so much, and proud of my sister and her entertaining and friendly ways.

Jane made a cup of coffee when she'd finished measuring Rose for the frock, then packed the two kids outside with a piece of chocolate cake each. We were sitting having coffee when we heard a truck turn in at the bottom of Frazers' drive.

Jane said, 'That's Alan. He's been down the road getting the Maoris for scrub cutting.'

I felt my face get hot. I was angry. At the same time I was hoping Rose would let the remark pass. I tried hard to think of something to say to cover Jane's words though I'd hardly said a thing all morning. But my tongue seemed to thicken and all I could think of was Rohe don't.

Rose was calm. Not all red and flustered like me. She took a big pull on the cigarette she had lit, squinted her eyes up and blew the smoke out gently. I knew something was coming.

'Don't they have names?'

'What. Who?' Jane was surprised and her face was getting pink.

'The people from down the road whom your husband is employing to cut scrub.' Rose the stink thing, she was talking all Pakehafied.

'I don't know any of their names.'

I was glaring at Rose because I wanted her to stop but she was avoiding my looks and pretending to concentrate on her cigarette.

'Do they know yours?'

'Mine?'

'Your name.'

'Well . . . Yes.'

'Yet you have never bothered to find out their names or to wonder whether or not they have any.'

The silence seemed to bang around in my head for ages and ages. Then I think Jane muttered something about difficulty, but that touchy sister of mine stood up and said,

'Come on Hera.' And I with my red face and shut mouth followed her out to the station wagon without a goodbye or anything.

I was so wild with Rose. I was wild. I was determined to blow her up about what she had done, I was determined. But now that we were alone together I couldn't think what to say. Instead I felt an awful big sulk coming on. It has always been my trouble, sulking. Whenever I don't feel sure about something I go into a big fat sulk. We had a teacher at school who used to say to some of us girls, 'Speak, don't sulk.' She'd say, 'You only sulk because you haven't learned how and when to say your minds.'

She was right that teacher, yet here I am a young woman about to be married and haven't learned yet how to get the words out. Dad used to say to me, 'Look out girlie, you'll stand on your lip.'

At last I said, 'Rose, you're a stink thing.' Tears were on the way. 'Gee Rohe, you made me embarrassed.' Then Rose said, 'Don't worry Honey she's got a thick hide.'

These words of Rose's took me by surprise and I realised something about Rose then. What she said made all my anger go away and I felt very sad because it's not our way of talking to each other. Usually we'd say, 'Never mind Sis,' if we wanted something to be forgotten. But when Rose said, 'Don't worry Honey she's got a thick hide,' it made her seem a lot older than me, and tougher, and as though she knew much more than me about the world. It made me realise too that underneath her jolly and forthright ways Rose is very hurt. I remembered back to when we were both little and Rose used to play up at school if she didn't like the teacher. She'd get smart and I used to be ashamed and tell Mum on her when we got home, because although she had the brains I was always the well behaved one.

Rose was speaking to me in a new way now. It made me feel sorry for her and for myself. All my life I had been sitting back and letting her do the objecting. Not only me, but

Mum and Dad and the rest of the family too. All of us too scared to make known when we had been hurt or slighted. And how can the likes of Jane know when we go round pretending all is well. How can Jane know us?

But then I tried to put another thought into words. I said to Rose, 'We do it too. We say, "the Pakeha doctor," or "the Pakeha at the post office", and sometimes we mean it in a bad way.'

'Except that we talk like this to each other only. It's not so much what is said, but when and where and in whose presence. Besides, you and I don't speak in this way now, not since we were little. It's the older ones: Mum, Dad, Nanny who have this habit.'

Then Rose said something else. 'Jane Frazer will still want to be your friend and mine in spite of my embarrassing her today; we're in the fashion.'

'What do you mean?'

'It's fashionable for a Pakeha to have a Maori for a friend.' Suddenly Rose grinned. Then I heard Jane's voice coming out of that Rohe's mouth and felt a grin of my own coming. 'I have friends who are Maoris. They're lovely people. The eldest girl was married recently and I did the frocks. The other girl is at varsity. They're all so *friendly* and so *natural* and their house is absolutely *spotless*.'

I stopped the wagon in the drive and when we'd got out Rose started strutting up the path. I saw Jane's way of walking and felt a giggle coming on. Rose walked up Mum's scrubbed steps, 'Absolutely spotless.' She left her shoes in the porch and bounced into the kitchen. 'What did I tell you? Absolutely spotless. And a friendly natural woman taking new bread from the oven.'

Mum looked at Rose then at me. 'What have you two been up to? Rohe I hope you behaved yourself at that Pakeha place?' But Rose was setting the table. At the sight of Mum's bread she'd forgotten all about Jane and the events of the morning.

When Dad, Heke, and Matiu came in for lunch, Rose, Mum, Nanny and I were already into the bread and the big bowl of hot corn.

'E ta,' Dad said. 'Let your hardworking father and your two hardworking brothers starve. Eat up.'

'The bread's terrible. You men better go down to the shop and get you a shop bread,' said Rose.

'Be the day,' said Heke.

'Come on my fat Rohe. Move over and make room for your Daddy. Come on my baby shift over.'

Dad squeezed himself round behind the table next to Rose. He picked up the bread Rose had buttered for herself and started eating. 'The bread's terrible all right,' he said. Then Mat and Heke started going on about how awful the corn was and who cooked it and who grew it, who watered it all summer and who pulled out the weeds.

So I joined in the carryings on and forgot about Rose and Jane for the meantime. But I'm not leaving it at that. I'll find some way of letting Rose know I understand and I know it will be difficult for me because I'm not clever the way she is. I can't say things the same and I've never learnt to stick up for myself.

But my sister won't have to be alone again. I'll let her know that.

TOKI

From the north he came, Toki, in his young day. Ah yes. A boaster this one, Toki the fisherman.

'They are all there, the fish,' he said. 'In the waters of the north. The tamure, the tarakihi, the moki, and the hapuku. And Toki, he has the line and the hand for all of them,' Toki from the north, Toki the fisherman.

But it was not as a fisherman we saw him then but as a boaster and a stranger, and looked upon with suspicion by many. And named Toki Fish by us since long ago days.

Long ago we had a mind for the same girl, Toki and I. A beautiful girl this, and looking my way till he came with his boasting ways. Promised to me, for it had been arranged between our families. Then he came, Toki, and her head was turned until I showed him as a boaster.

After the wedding of my eldest brother when all were gathered for singing and dancing, he began to boast again of days fishing, Toki. To scorn our ways and these waters of ours. And she listened with eyes down, the girl, which was a way of hers. Very jealous then I, and stood to speak.

'Well it may be,' I said, 'to catch many fish where fish are many. In the north they are plenty, the fish, and you wait with your hooks and your lines for them to come. A fisherman of skill catches fish where there are none to catch.'

'They are many or they are few, the fish,' said Toki. 'Still they come to me for I have the line and the hand.'

'Together then we, tomorrow,' I replied, and he knew my meaning as did those who listened.

'Not together, but one, then the other,' he.

'Together tomorrow to choose the place,' I. 'After that I go, and the next day you.'

They all spoke then, the old people, of days fishing, and much advice they gave to we of young days. But sat quietly, I, to wait for morning. Then rowed together past the point of crayfish rock and in a line with Poroti where green meets blue.

'Here then,' I said.

'So,' said Toki.

It was all there, the bait, when we returned, for all were eager to see who would be the fisherman of skill. To the rocks for crayfish they, for it is best bait in these parts.

Next morning then I, with many there early to see me go. Out to sea with the day just coming, pulling strong and straight. Around the point, then quickly to the chosen place to get down my line before sunrise.

Not one of the good fishing grounds this, and doubtful at the start. But as the day came in the tarakihi. A quick pull this, and knew many would follow because it is the way of the tarakihi. Eight hooks to my line, and counted eight before bringing it up. Fat they were, waving in the water as my hand pulled in my line. Quick to put on my bait again and put it at the bottom of the sea, for it feeds quickly the tarakihi. Four times to the surface with eight, and a good beginning. But the time after this, pulling the line, there came the heads of my tarakihi but not the bodies. Gone. The work of a hapuku this, and very excited then I.

Quickly to change the bottom hooks for a bigger size and tie the bait on firmly.

'Come to me hapuku,' I said. 'Come to me old man. Come to the line of Hotene. This is the line for you and this the bait.'

My hand felt the pull of the tarakihi many times but

waited. Then away, the line, with the strong slow pull of the hapuku.

'Mine then,' I said, and brought him up. A big size, though it was not the grounds of the hapuku.

Then at the slacking of the water, rolled in my line to rest and prepare my spinner, for it is the time of the blind eel, this.

Not many more fish for me that day, but knew my catch was good for such a place of chance. Home then, hard pulling with my paua shell spinner flashing at the back of the boat, waiting for the eye of the kahawai. Round the corner it waited, the kahawai, and a spread of green and silver as it took the spinner.

A happy fisherman then, I, heading for home to the crowd on the beach. A lucky day this, and knew I'd not be beaten. But then it was, as I waited for the eighth wave to take me in, that I thought of what could happen. He sees all these fish of mine, Toki, and he will know he cannot equal in such a place chosen. He will go then, well out to sea, to the grounds of the hapuku. There to fish because his boast is strong.

Now in these parts the landing of a boat is not safe except to come in on the eighth wave. Watch for the biggest, then after this, turn your boat into the eighth. It is the right size this one to take your boat to the shallows safely. Kept from the ears of Toki, it would be my safeguard, this.

To the hills early next morning, and from there saw the little boat head straight for the deep. Glad then that I had kept the secret of the waves.

Many were there to watch him come in and so sat quietly to watch. No counting of waves Toki, but turned his boat into a breaker of small size which brought him halfway in. But then came the big one. A big one this, swelling and getting faster, up to the boat, then...crash!

Swamped, the boat, and Toki in the water with his catch around him as I had thought. Toki Fish we named him as he swam for shore and that has been his name since. All were happy for me to show him as a boaster, because all knew he had not gone to the chosen place to fish. And she came to my side once more, the girl, and is there still though old lady now, she.

He goes for the paua and the kina now, Toki. He throws his line from the beach for the shark, but no more in a boat he, for fear of what would be said. But a boaster still this one, a boaster still. It blows strong the wind from north.

AT THE RIVER

Sad I wait, and see them come slow back from the river.
The torches move slow.

To the tent to rest after they had gone to the river, and
while asleep the dream came. A dream of death. He came
to me in the dream, not sadly but smiling, with hand on
heart and said, 'I go but do not weep. No weeping, it is my
time.'

Woke then and out into the night to watch for them with
sadness on me, sadness from the dream. And waiting, there
came a morepork with soft wing beat and rested above my
head. 'Go,' I said to the bird. 'He comes not with you tonight. He is well and strong. His time is not here.'

But it cried, the morepork. Its call went out. Out and out
until the tears were on my face. And now I wait and I see the
torches come, they move slow back from the river. Slow and
sad they move and I think of him.

Many times have we come to this place for eels. Every
year we come at this time. Our children come, and now our
grandchildren, his and mine. This is the river for eels and
this the time of year.

A long way we have travelled with our tents and food
stores, our lamps and bedding and our big eel drums. Much
work for us today preparing our camp. But now our camp is
ready and they have gone with the torches down river to the
best eel place. And this old lady stays behind with her old

kerosene lamp and the camp fire dying, and the little ones sleeping in their beds. Too tired for the river tonight, too old for the work of catching eels. But not he. He is well and strong. No aching back or tired arms he. No bending, no sadness on him or thoughts of death like this old one.

His wish but not mine to come here this year. 'Too old,' I said to him. 'Let the young ones go. Stay back we two and tend our kumara and corn.'

'This old body,' he said. 'It hungers for the taste of eel.'

'The drums will be full when they return,' I said. 'Let them bring the eels to us, as they would wish to do.'

'Ah no,' he said. 'Always these hands have fetched the food for the stomach. The eels taste sweeter when the body has worked in fetching.'

'Go then,' I said, and we prepared.

I think of him now as I await their return. 'My time is here,' he said in the dream, and now the bird calls out. And I think too of the young ones who spoke to him today in a new way, a way I did not like.

Before the night came they worked, all of them, to make their torches for the river. Long sticks of manuka, long and straight. Tins tied at the tops of the sticks, and in the tins rag soaked in oil. A good light they made as they left tonight for the river. Happy and singing they went with their torches. But I see the lights return now, dim. Dim and slow they come and sadly I await them.

And the young ones, they made their eel hooks. Straight sticks with strong hooks tied for catching eels. He smiled to see the eel hooks, the straight sticks with the strong hooks tied.

'Your hooks,' he said, 'they work for the hands?' But the young ones did not speak, instead bent heads to the work of tying hooks.

Then off, the young ones, to the hills for hare bait as the sun went down. Happy they went with the gun. Two shots went out and we awaited their return. The young ones, they came back laughing. Happy they came with the hare. 'Good bait this,' they said. 'Good bait and good hooks. Lots of eels for us tonight.'

But their nanny said to them, 'A hook is good for the eel but bad for the leg. Many will be there at the river to-night, your uncles, aunties, big cousins, your nanny too. Your hooks may take a leg in place of an eel. The old way, with the stick, and the bait tied is a safe way and a good way. You waste your time with hooks.'

But the young ones rolled on the ground. 'Ho Grandpa,' they called. 'You better watch your leg tonight. The hook might get your leg Grandpa.'

'And watch your hand Grandpa, the eel might get your hand.'

'Bite your hand off Grandpa. You better watch out.'

Did not like their way of talking to their nanny but he has patience with the young.

'You'll see,' he said. 'You want to know how to get eels then you watch your Grandpa.'

They did not keep quiet, the young ones after that. Called out to him in a way I did not like, but he is patient.

'Ah Grandpa, that old way of yours is no good. That way is old like you Grandpa.'

'You might end up in the river with your old way of catching eels.'

Spoke sharply to them then in our own language.

'Not for you to speak in this manner. Not our way to speak like this. It is a new thing you are doing. It is a bad thing you have learned.'

No more talk from these two then, but laughing still, and he spoke up for them.

'They make their torches, the boys, and they make the hooks, and then they go to the hills for hare. They think of the river and the eels in the river, and then they punch each other and roll on the ground. Shout and laugh waiting for the night to come. The funny talk it means nothing.'

'Enough to shout and fight,' I said. 'Enough to roll on the ground and punch each other, but the talk needs to stay in the mouth.'

Put my head down then not pleased, and worked at my task of kneading the bread for morning.

Now I wait and stir the ashes round the oven while the morning bread cooks, and on the ashes I see my tears fall. The babies sleep behind me in the tent, and above me the bird cries.

Much to do after a night of eeling when the drum is full. From the fire we scrape away the dead ashes to put into the drum of eels. All night our eels stay there in the drum of ashes to make easier the task of scraping. Scrape off the ashes and with them come the sticky eel slime. Cut the eels, and open them out then ready for smoking. The men collect green manuka for our smoke drum. Best wood this, to make a good smoke. Good and clean. All day our smoke house goes. Then wrap our smoked eel carefully and pack away before night comes and time for the river again.

But no eels for us this night. No scraping and smoking and packing this time. Tonight our camp comes down and we return. The dim lights come and they bring him back from the river. Slow they bring him.

Now I see two lights come near. The two have come to bring me sad news of him. But before them the bird came, and before the bird the dream—he in the dream with hand on heart.

And now they stand before me, the boys, heads down. By the dim torch light I see the tears on their faces, they do not speak.

'They bring your nanny back,' I say. 'Back from the river.' But they do not speak.

'Hear the morepork,' I say to them. 'It calls from the trees. Out and out it cries. They bring him back from the river, I see your tears.'

'We saw him standing by the river,' they say. 'Saw him

bend, looking into the water, and then we saw him fall.'

They stand, the young ones in the dim torch-light with tears on their faces, the tears fall. And now they come to me, kneeling by me, weeping.

'We spoke bad to him,' they say. 'They were bad things we said. Now he has fallen and we have said bad things to him.'

So I speak to them to comfort them. 'He came to me to-night with hand on heart. "Do not weep," he said. "It is my time." Not your words that made him fall. His hand was on his heart. Hear the morepork cry. His time is here.'

And now we weep together, this old lady and these two young ones by her. No weeping he said. But we will weep a little while for him and for ourselves. He was our strength.

We weep and they return. His children and mine return from the river bearing him. Sad they come in the dim light of torches. The young ones help me to my feet, weeping still, and I go towards them as they come.

And in my throat I feel a cry well up. Lonely it sounds across the night. Lonely it sounds, the cry that comes from in me.

TRANSITION

See what they do, these grandsons and granddaughters of mine. Take these large stones from the river bed and put them here on the track where each day I walk. This is what they do, these mokopuna, and so to please them I walk with the bad leg that has in it a feeling of deadness. This way and that, round and about the big river stones to make these young ones happy.

Home from school they will say to me, 'Did you walk today Nanny? Did you see our stones, our big river stones?'

'Yes,' I will say. 'Yes, I walked. This way and that. Round and about the stones making the old leg all tired,'

'Ah Nanny. Soon we will have your leg all better. Soon. You'll see Nanny.'

And then seeing how pleased they are, I will be happy to have done this for them. Not much time left now to give happiness to these little ones. Soon this old light goes out.

And the mother too. This daughter of mine. Every morning this daughter gives me the work of kneading bread in order to get the lame hand strong once more. Sad this daughter. Sad to see this old one hobble about with one side lame. And sad this old one to see the daughter with yet another worry on her.

I tell her, never mind. Never mind this old one. Look to the young. Look to the years ahead.

And yet this one asks herself what future there is for these dear ones of hers.

And a great sadness comes.

What future on this little corner of land, once enough to support many but now in these days merely a worry and a trouble. The ground dry and hard, and great round stones where once a river flowed. A great sadness comes, for this old one knows that soon these ones must go away from this place. The city must claim these loved ones of hers, and in claiming take its price. But nowhere for this old one in such a new place. Her place is here, and so the daughter has a sadness on her.

'Come,' she says. 'Come with your children. We cannot leave you here. Before when you were well, though not even then happily. But now, since your illness?'

'Each day,' I say, 'I am a little stronger. Here I can walk along beside the river bed. Still I can take a hoe in one good hand, still I can roll the dough for new bread, and have others here beside me. My needs are few.'

But she is torn in two this daughter.

I say to her, 'Here is the place where I was born and here is where I die.'

And the mokopuna who listen say, 'Don't talk so funny Nanny.' So I try to tell them there is nothing to fear.

'No need to fear a life ahead without an old Nanny. This is just an old Nanny with her light getting dim who likes to see her days go by in this house, on this poor dried out piece of land where she was born.'

Then the husband, father of these little ones stands firm and says, 'We cannot leave you here and if you'll not come then we stay too. This wife of mine and these children would fret away in the town without their old lady.'

'Go,' I say. 'Here there is nothing.'

'And there?' he asks, and I know his meaning.

'The arrangements are made,' I say to him, 'And you must go.'

'Made before your illness,' he says, 'And now can be unmade.' The mokopuna listen and are glad, and the daughter too.

'We can get along,' she says. 'We have till now, and shall. This is a better place, a freer place, and our hearts are here.'

Look then at this daughter of mine, ageing before her time with so much work, and this good son-in-law with the worry of bills to be paid and future needs to look to. Then the children much too thin, and the older ones with little time for school work because of chores. A great sadness.

Yet suddenly all these ones of mine are smiling, laughing because the good son-in-law has said arrangements can be unmade, and they will stay here with the old Nanny on the dried up place.

'Ha Nanny,' they say. 'We will stay here with you now and make your leg better with our rocks. You'll see Nanny.'

'And cook special food for you as the doctor said so you can live to a hundred.'

All at once this old one is laughing too. 'Better for an old Nanny like this to keep her old habits and go away happy, than live to a hundred on dried up kai.'

Away then happy to their jobs. Laughing, and happy to work till dark on this thirsting soil, and leaving this old one minding the days gone past. Not long now for the light grows dim. Not long now will this old woman hold these ones here, for soon this light goes out. These ones of hers will go from this place with some sadness, remembering an old lady that once was their bond. But yet will depart with a new hope coming and a new life to make.

This old one awaits that time, which is not long away. Not long. Then this old body goes to this old ground, and the two shall be one, with no more to be given by one or by the other to those who weep.

And from the two—the land, the woman—these ones have sprung. And by the land and by the woman held and strengthened. Now, from knowing this, the old one in turn draws strength as the old light dims, as the time of passing comes.

THE DREAM

It was still dark when Raniera awoke from a disturbed sleep. In the night the dream had come to him. Carefully he groped back through the fuzz of his awakening, pushing his thoughts back into the dark moments of oblivion. The dream...what was it now? He had seen himself in his dream. Alone—standing on the soft bank of a deep muddy creek. Stooping, peering into the murky water, and something in his hand...a rope.

Yes, a rope. Now it all came to him...the hinaki. His hinaki, sucked deep into the soft grey mud, and himself pulling on the rope knowing that the hinaki would be full of eels, because pulling took all his strength.

Slowly the wire cage had surfaced and he had seen that it was full, not with several eels as he had thought, but with one big eel—thick, black, coiled round in the hinaki like an inflated inner tube.

And in the dream he had dragged his hinaki with the eel in it up the bank, and tipped the eel out on the grass... the biggest eel he had ever seen. He had seen himself stoop over the eel, put a hand under each gill, and push his fingers around its slimy girth until his fingers touched under the belly. Then he had pointed his thumbs together over the eel's back and his thumbs had just touched.

There the dream had ended—with him stooping over the eel and measuring its girth with his hands. A hand on each side, thumbs touching, fingers touching.

This, he felt, was the important part of his dream. What did it mean? He felt under the pillow for his *Best Bets,* then reached out to light the candle which was on a chair by the bed.

Best Bets was open at the second leg. Slowly he read down the list of names, turning each carefully in his mind—looking for a connection with his dream.

Gay Ring
Prophecy
Gold Stripe
Fair Fellow
Nothing about eels there.
. . . Lonely Boy—lonely? Alone? He had been alone in his dream.
. . . Black Knight—the eel was black, the creek dark. . .
Black Knight?
. . . Prophecy—hadn't he tried to prophesy what was in the hinaki? But he had been wrong, and that meant Prophecy wouldn't win. He scratched a line through Prophecy with the burnt match-head.
Blue Smoke
Dark Beauty
Royal Sun
Lucky Touch
Guardian
Foxwood.

He went over the dream again in his mind, then he put the book down, cupped his fingers together, tipped thumbs. A big eel. As big as that. There must be a winner there somewhere. He'd better get to town early to see Ben and the others, and they could all talk about the dream. Work it out. Must be a winner there somewhere.

'E Hika! He aha te moemoea?' called Ben as Raniera stepped from the taxi and waved to the driver.
'What's the dream?'
'E tama, he tuna.'

'Ei! Kia tika ra!'

'Yeh! A big one this eel. Ka nui te kaita!'

He showed Ben with his hands the size of the eel of his dream. And there under the white verandah of the T.A.B. his friends gathered to listen; Ben, Lucy, Monty, Hone, Ritimana, Haua.

Raniera told them how he had been stooping, looking into the mud. They watched him carefully as he showed them how he had pulled the hinaki in, pulled it up the bank, tipped the eel on to the grass.

'Wii!' he said. 'A big eel—that size.' And he showed them how he had measured it with his hands...fingers touching under the belly, thumbs touching over the back.

'Pai, Good dream ne?' said Haua.

'E champion.'

They nodded, smiled, and turned the pages of *Best Bets*; studied the second leg.

'One eel,' said Lucy. 'Number one, Gay Ring. One eel. Number one'.

'Dark Beauty,' said Ben. 'A beauty eel. Dark. Dark Beauty!' One by one they gave their opinions and advice.

At last it was eleven o'clock, time to place bets for the double. Into the pastel painted room they went and had a final look at the printed lists on the wall. Up to the window. Bets placed.

Raniera gave his numbers. 'Twelve,' he said. No trouble there. His daughter Rose had turned twelve two days ago. Number twelve, Sunset Rose, but the second? 'Aee,' he sighed. One eel in the hinaki, and the eel coiled in a ring. Number one, Gay Ring, Must be. 'Twelve and one,' he said.

There was a hush in the bar as the race began. 'This ti--ime,' called the commentator. 'Off to a good start...Fair Fellow, Guardian, Gay Ring.'

Raniera, Ben, Monty, Hone, Ritimana, and Haua drummed their fists on the bar.

'Na, Gay Ring.'

'Ho! A good start. Ka pai ne?'

Earlier that day they had heard Sunset Rose come in, and now they listened eagerly, certain that this was to be Raniera's lucky day. 'E champion, this dream,' they said.

As the race progressed they all pressed closely together at the bar, feet tapping, bodies rocking.

'Kia kaha! Gay Ring,' they called as Gay Ring went through to challenge the leading horse.

'My horse that one. My dream,' shouted Raniera.

But Gay Ring, after going into the lead and holding it for a short while, began to tire.

'Gay Ring dropping well back now,' called the commentator.

'Aue!'

'Kei whea Gay Ring?'

Shoulders drooped, elbows pressed onto the bar, heads shook slowly.

'And as they pass the post it's Lucky Touch half a length from Gold Stripe, two lengths to Lonely Boy...'

'E tama. Kei whea to moemoea? What happened to the dream?'

'Aue! No good.'

Once again out came *Best Bets*. Fingers down the list— Lucky Touch. Number ten. Lucky Touch.

'Aue!' said Ben, and he flicked his arms above his head. 'Number Ten.' And as the others nodded, sighed, he explained. 'Five fingers on this hand. And five fingers on this hand.' He showed them his hands. 'E Ra,' he turned to Raniera. 'You put your hands around the tuna like this. Na? Five and five are ten—Number ten. The fingers touched - Lucky Touch, the fingers touched.'

'Aee,' they agreed.

'Ko tera taku! I'll say!'

Raniera shook his head. 'Aue! Waste a good dream.'

'No dough for the Maori today,' said Monty. 'Ka hinga ta tatau crate.'

They all laughed.

'E ta, ko haunga to tuna,' said Ritimana slicing the air with his hand. 'Your eel stinks.'

'Na! Ka puta mai te piro,' called Haua, as the laughter rose.

Then Raniera spread his fingers wide, raised both arms above his head, 'Whio!' he yelled. Down came his arms in a full arm sweep. 'Haunga!'

'Haunga!' they echoed, and their laughter swelled, burst, and filled the bar.

HOLIDAY

You know, I love my Nanny Retimana. Every holidays I say to Mum and Daddy, I'm going to my Nanny Retimana's, and I pack my bag. And Mum and Daddy take me down to the railway station and put me in the railcar, and even though it's a long, long way to Nanny Retimana's place I don't care. I wouldn't care if Nanny lived on the other side of the world or up on the moon, I'd still go every holidays to see her.

Mum and Daddy put me in the railcar with some sandwiches and apples and comics, and they kiss me and tell me everything to do and everything not to do. Then they kiss me again and wave. And it is a little bit sad to go away from Mum and Daddy, especially when they worry and keep telling me this and that. But they shouldn't worry because I'm so happy to go to Nanny Retimana's and I know everything to do and everything not to do. And all the way in the railcar my Nanny Retimana's name keeps going round and round in my head like music—Nanny Retimana, Nanny Retimana. And Papa Retimana too of course. I love him too even though he cheeks me a lot.

Nanny and Papa have an old car, and Papa won't let anyone drive it but him. He goes everywhere in his old car. To town, to the pub, to football; to Wellington, Auckland, anywhere. One day he even went over the bank in it, with Nanny and my two Aunties and Uncle Charlie, all the shopping and his beer and me. Roll, roll, bang the car went, and landed on its side on the creek road below the bank. And I was sitting on top of Auntie Materoa who was on top of Uncle Charlie who has a stiff leg. I was glad I wasn't underneath because you should see how fat Auntie Materoa and Uncle Charlie are.

None of us was hurt very much, but the eggs were all smashed and Papa Retimana got hit on the back of the neck with a tin of golden syrup. And Auntie Kiri was all spooky because the bag of flour broke and she had white eyebrows and eyelashes and a white chin. And she was sneezing all the time.

We all had to climb up out of the window, which was a tight squeeze for everyone but me, and Uncle Charlie couldn't get out at all because of his stiff leg. So Auntie Kiri had to get back in and push him up while the others pulled. Auntie Kiri was still sneezing too, and it took a long time to get Uncle Charlie out.

Gee, and the car was all dented and the shopping was everywhere. Eggs, flour, rolled oats, potatoes. Everywhere. But, you know, Papa's beer was all right. Not one bottle was broken and Papa was really happy. Auntie Kiri looked at the beer and she looked at Papa's happy face and said, 'E ta! The devil looks after his own. Hard case all right.' But Papa didn't care about her teasing because he was so glad about his beer.

Nanny and Papa Retimana always come down in their car to meet me at the station. I watch out the window and I see the two of them there and I'm glad because they look just the same as ever. I get out of the railcar and I go and hug them both, and you know, Papa Retimana nearly breaks all my bones with his big hug. I ride all the way back to Nanny's place squashed between my Nanny and Papa, and they say to me, 'Ah you still skinny Atareta', and they shake their heads. And they say, 'Ah your mummy been cutting your hair', and they shake their heads again. But I don't really think they mind how skinny I am, I don't think they're really angry about my short hair, they squeeze me all the way back to their place for thirty miles. And, you

know, my name isn't Atareta at all. My name's Lynette.
But Nanny says I look just like my Auntie Atareta who lives
way down the South Island and who I've never seen. And
when my Auntie Atareta was little she used to sit on her legs
with her feet sticking out at the sides the same as I do. Well
that's what Nanny Retimana says, and Nanny Retimana,
she calls me Atareta all the time.

When we come to Nanny and Papa's little house I see that
it's just the same as the last time and I feel really glad. I
like Nanny and Papa Retimana's house, all painted white
with the little paths running everywhere. The paths are all
covered in stones and shells, and all the flower gardens are
edged by big round river stones that Nanny and Papa have
painted all colours. And it looks so cheerful always. I like
arriving at Nanny and Papa's and seeing all the pretty paths
and gardens, all the bright painted stones, and the little
white house sitting in amongst it all.

When we get inside Nanny gets me a whole lot of kai out
of the big pot on the stove so she can make me fat. And it's
a wonder I'm not as fat as anything because I eat everything
Nanny gives me, and I have bread and a big mug of tea as
well. Papa cuts off thick slices of Nanny's bread for him and
me. He puts thick butter on his bread and then he dips it in
his tea. 'That's the way,' he says. 'Bread on butter and put
it in the tea.' So I do it too and it's good, you know. It's a
wonder I'm not as fat as anything.

After I've had my kai I go into Nanny's sitting room and
look at all of her and Papa's photos.

'All your relations Atareta,' Nanny tells me. And she
talks to me about all my old nannies who are dead now,
and my aunties and uncles and cousins. There are photos
of me there too with Mum and Daddy, and one of Mum
and Daddy's wedding. And some of Auntie Atareta
and her husband and kids who live way down the South
Island. Some of the photos are hard case too, like the one of
my cousin Danny pulling an ugly face, and the one of

Uncle Charlie asleep out on the grass and all you can see in the photo is Uncle's big puku sticking up.

I'm always glad to go to bed after my long journey in the railcar, so after Nanny and I have looked at all the photos I change and get into my bed with the three mattresses on and go fast asleep.

Most days there's just Nanny and Papa and me, and I help them with the work and talk a lot. I help Nanny with the dishes and we polish the lino, and sometimes we make jam or bottle some fruit.

I like to go out and help Papa too. We feed all the ducks, and Papa's old pig, and his two dogs, and in the afternoons we often go out to the gardens and work there.

But in the weekends we have to be quick with our jobs because that's when all my aunties and uncles and cousins start turning up. And my aunties look at me and say, 'Ah that's you Atareta,' and they all kiss me and so do my uncles. Then all my cousins kiss me too, so it's no wonder I don't get fat after all because I'm sure I get worn out after a while. But I still like it. I like all my aunties and uncles and cousins coming.

And I get out and play with my cousins. We ride the horse or go swimming in the river, or slide down the hills and wear our pants out. We play all day long until dark, and when we go back inside we're so hungry we eat everything out of the big pot and all the bread as well. Nanny and Papa Retimana and our aunties and uncles all have some beer and laugh a lot and talk, and Auntie Materoa, well she can't stop laughing. She laughs all the time. She sounds just like a fire engine with her way of laughing, 'Eeee Hardcase, Hardcase, Eeeeee,' with tears all running down. Uncle Ben teases her and says, 'You lay an egg in a minute Mattie.' And away Auntie Materoa goes again, 'Eeee Hardcase, Hardcase Eeeeee.'

Sometimes in the weekends instead of our aunties and uncles coming, we get in the car and go to one of their places. I like going to Auntie Kiri's place because it's not far from the beach. And you know, Auntie Kiri's house is really neat. It's flash. Auntie's place is all full of carpets and thick curtains and electric heaters, and a big TV, a deep freeze, clothes drier, and stereogram. Auntie's house is so flash she won't let us kids inside when we've been out playing until we've had a good wash under the hose.

We met Auntie in town one Friday and she told us to come back and stay with them so we did. It was raining that day. And when we got to Auntie's house Uncle Ben was sitting in the kitchen and Auntie's big clothes drier was rumbling away in the wash house. Auntie was really pleased with Uncle for doing all her washing and putting it in the drier and she gave him a big kiss.

Then afterwards she went to get the clothes out and she started yelling her head off out in the wash house,

'Parengo. Your stink parengo! Who told you to put your haunga seaweed in my drier?'

And Uncle said, 'How else do I dry my parengo in this weather?'

And we all ran out to the wash house to look at Uncle's parengo in Auntie's drier. Auntie Materoa who was there too started up laughing as usual, 'Eeee Hardcase, Parengo Eeeeee,' screeching, looking into Auntie Kiri's drier.

Gee Auntie Kiri growled. She called Uncle a stink and a dead loss and a taurekareka. Then after a while she started up laughing too, and Auntie Kiri's laugh is nearly as bad as Auntie Materoa's, well that's what I think.

Auntie Kiri can growl you know. She doesn't growl at us little kids though, only if we mess up her house, but she growls at her big grown up kids, my big married cousins. They always come there and start looking in the cupboards and all round the house for Auntie's bread.

'You made a bread Mum?' they say.

'You got any meat? Gee-ee Macky forgot to get us a meat for the weekend.' And Auntie Kiri growls.

'Don't you come here looking for bread and meat you tahae things,' she growls. But I don't think she means it really because afterwards she goes and gets the bread from a tin in her wardrobe and we all have some. And my big cousins all grin and say, 'Gee what a lovely bread Mum. Cunning all right.' And Auntie Kiri looks pleased and says, 'Cunning yourself.'

She growls too if they come to her place untidy. Mostly my cousins make sure to change before they come to Auntie's, but one day Benjy came in his old kanukanu pants and Auntie went off at him.

'Haven't you got a decent pants?' she said. 'Can't that fat wife of yours sew a button on your pants. Where is she anyway? At home with her eyes on the TV the lazy. You bring your wife next time, and bring my mokopuna. You didn't bring my mokopuna to see me.'

Then Auntie made a funny noise at Benjy to show how bad he was, "A-ack!"

Later that night when I was pretending to be asleep on the settee I heard Auntie saying, 'Come here useless,' to Benjy, and I peeped through my eyelashes and saw her with a needle and cotton and a button, and she started sewing a button on my big cousin's pants. And Benjy was dancing up and down saying, 'Gee-ee, look out Mum. Watch out you'll sew up my thing in a minute,' Rude ay?

But Auntie just said, 'Good job too,' and kept on sewing.

And of course Auntie Materoa started up screeching again. You know Auntie Materoa's hard case with her laugh. I had to wriggle down under my blanket so no one would see my mouth grinning.

I like going to Auntie Materoa's too. I don't sleep on the settee at Auntie Materoa's, I just get in bed with all her kids. My cousins and I get up to all sorts at Auntie Materoa's. We have pillow fights, and use the beds for trampolines, and dress up in Auntie Materoa's clothes and put her shoes on. Four of us can fit in one of Auntie Materoa's dresses, that's how fat Auntie Materoa is. And nobody growls. Nobody takes any notice of us kids yelling and jumping around in the bedroom. Even when we sneak out in the kitchen and have a feed they take no notice at all. They all sit round in Auntie Materoa's sitting room and drink their beer and sing. And they dance and do the hula, even my Nanny Retimana who is quite old really. She does the hula and they all shout hard case things to her like,

'Good on you aunt.'

'Swing it kuia.'

'Watch out, ka makare to tarau,' and that's just about rude because it means Nanny might lose her pants if she does the hula too much.

Nanny Retimana doesn't care, she shouts out, 'Shut up you fullas jealous, *E puru tai tama . . .* '

They all sing *E puru tai tama*, and start clapping and sometimes Uncle Charlie gets up and joins in the hula, and that sets Auntie Materoa off again because Uncle Charlie's got a stiff leg, 'Hardcase! Hardcase!' tears running down and us kids all looking round the door to watch Uncle Charlie and Nanny Retimana and some others doing the hula.

I enjoy myself at my Auntie Kiri's and Auntie Materoa's, but I'm always pleased to get back to Nanny's where we can be peaceful and quiet again, and I go round helping Nanny and Papa and play with the ducks and Papa's two dogs, or have a quiet ride on the horse.

And my holiday never seems very long. It's soon time to pack my bag again and get into Papa Retimana's old car - it's still got all the dents in too and there's a stain on the seat where all the syrup poured out - and Nanny and Papa take me to the station and put me in the railcar with some kai in a biscuit tin, and some pauas in a plastic bag from Auntie Kiri to the take home to Mum and Daddy.

I wave to my Nanny and Papa Retimana out of the rail-car window. I wave and wave until I can't see them any more, and I'm sorry to be going away from them. Then after a while I start thinking about Mum and Daddy waiting for me at the other end, but it seems a long, long way. I have a few sleeps, and I nibble at all the kai Nanny Retimana has packed for me. Then as I get nearer to home I start to feel excited because Mum and Daddy will be waiting at the station for me. Then I think what if they've changed? What if they're different or don't know me? And I worry and put my face to the window as the railcar comes in, and I see them both standing on the platform waiting for me. And I see they haven't changed. They're not different at all, and they do know me because they start smiling when they see my face at the window.

You know, I love Mum and Daddy. I pick up my bag and my tin of kai and my pauas in a plastic bag from Auntie Kiri, and I hurry out of the railcar and onto the platform. I hug Mum and Daddy and we go and get into our car. I sit between them on the front seat and they squeeze me all the way home to our place.

WAIARIKI

When we were little boys we often used to go around the beach for kai moana. And when we reached the place where the rocks were we'd always put our kits down on the sand and mimi on them so the shellfish would be plentiful.

Whenever the tides were good we would get our kits and sugar-bags and knives ready, then go up at the back of our place to catch the horses—Blue Pony, Punch, Creamy, and Crawford. And people who lived inland would ring and ask us about the tides. 'He aha te tai?' they'd ask over the phone—'What time's the tide?' and we'd tell them. All morning the phone would ring; 'He aha te tai? He aha te tai?'

And on those days there would be crowds of us going round the beach on horses with our kits and knives, and when we arrived at the place for gathering shellfish we boys would mimi on our kits and sugar bags then wash them in the salt water, all of us hoping for plenty of kai moana to take home.

We never thought much about the quiet beauty of the place where we lived then. Not in the way I have thought about it since. I have many times wished I could be there, living again, in our house overlooking the long curve of beach and the wide expanse of sea. We could climb up through the plantation behind our place to the clearings at the top and look away out for miles, and could feel as free as the seagulls that hung in the wind above the water. It was from this hill that I once saw a whale out off the point, sending up plumes of spray as it travelled out to the deep. And on another occasion from the same hill, we watched the American fleet go by, all the ships fully lit, moving quietly past in the dusk.

If we went down the gully and up on the hills at the left we could look back to where our old house had been, then down to the present dwelling with all the flower gardens and trees around it. And below the house by the creek were our big vegetable gardens which kept us busy all year round. One would have thought that with vegetable gardens to tend, our parents would not have had time for flowers. But flowers, shrubs, and trees we had in abundance, and looking down from the hills, or from the beach below, the area round the house was always a mass of colour. But it is now, looking back, that I appreciate this more.

The bird tree was our favourite, with its scarlet flowers like red birds flying. Then there were the hibiscus of many different colours, the coral tree, kaka beak, and many varieties of coloured manuka and broom. And there was a big old rata under which one of our brothers was born, and named Rata for the tree.

In front of the house at the end of the lawn was a bank where scores of coloured cinerarias, blackeyed susans, and ice plants grew, and beyond there was the summer house that my father and brothers built before I was born. This was where my father had all his hanging baskets crowded with ferns and flowers.

When I first left there to go away to school, and when I first realised what other people had in the way of money and possessions, I used to think how poor we children were. I used to think about it and feel ashamed that our patched clothing, much of it army surplus, was the best we had. And felt ashamed that the shoes that had been bought for me for high school were my first and only pair. It wasn't until many years later that I realised that we had many of the good things, and all the necessary things of life.

There were ten of us living in the house at the time I remember, but there were older children who had married and gone away. Seventeen children my parents had altogether, though not all lived. I can remember the day my youngest sister and her twin were born. Our mother had been away at one of the top gardens getting puha, and on our way home from school we could see her coming down the track on Crawford. And our father was standing by the gate with his hands on his hips, shaking his head.

'That one riding on a horse,' he was saying. 'That one riding on a horse.'

And Mum got down off the horse when she got home and said, 'Oh Daddy, I was hungry for puha.' Then she began walking round and round the house, pressing her hands into her sides, pressing her hands. Later she went to bed and Dad delivered the girl.

My big sister Ngahuia brought the new little sister Maurea out into the kitchen where it was warm and began washing her. Then Mum called out to Dad that there was another baby and at first he thought it was all teka. He thought she was teasing because he had growled about her riding on the horse. But when he went to her he knew she wasn't playing after all and went to help, but the boy was stillborn. Mum was sad then because she had been riding on the horse so close to her time, but my father was good to her and said no, it was because the boy was too small. They took the tiny body up to where the old place had been, and buried it there with the other babies that had not lived.

Maurea was never very strong and on most nights we went to sleep listening to the harsh sound of her coughing. That was until she was about five years old. Then our parents took her to an old aunt of ours who knew about sicknesses, and the old aunt pushed her long forefinger down our sister's throat and hooked out lump after lump of hard knotted phlegm. Maurea was much better from then on though still prone to chest complaints and has never been sturdy like the rest of us.

There were three different places where we went for kai moana. The first, about a mile round the beach, called Huapapa, was a place of small lagoons and rock pools. The rocks here were large and flat and extended well out into the sea. This was a good place for kina and paua and pupu. We would ride the horses out as far as we could and tether them to a rock. They would stand there in the sun and go to sleep. To get kina we would go out to where the small waves were breaking, in water about knee deep. We'd peer into the water turning the flat stones over, and it wouldn't take long to fill a sugar bag with kina. The paua were there too, as well as in the rock pools further towards shore. The younger children who were not old enough to stand in the deeper water, and not strong enough to turn the big rocks for paua and kina, would look about in the rock pools for pupu, each one of them hoping to find the biggest and the best.

The next place, Karekare, further round the beach was also a good place for shellfish, but the reason we liked to go there was that there was a small lagoon with a narrow inlet, which was completely cut off from the sea at low tide. Often at low tide there were fish trapped there in the lagoon. And we children would all stand around the edge of the lagoon and throw rocks at the fish.

'Ana! Ana!' we'd yell

'Patua! Patua!' hurling the stones into the water. And usually there would be at least one fish floating belly up in the lagoon by the time we'd finished. Whoever jumped in first and grabbed it would keep it and take it home.

One day after a week of rain we arrived at Karekare to find the water in the lagoon brown and murky, and even before we got down from the horses we could see two dozen or more fins circling, breaking the surface of the water. We all got off the horses and ran out over the rocks calling, 'Mango, Mango,' and scrambled everywhere looking for rocks and stones to throw. But my father came out and told us to put the rocks down. Then he walked out into the lagoon and began reaching into the water. Suddenly he threw his arms up, and there was a shower of water, and a shark came spinning through the air, 'Mango, Mango,' way up over our heads with its white belly glistening and large drops of water raining all over us. 'Mango, Mango,' we shouted. Then—Smack! It landed threshing on the rocks behind us. So we hit it on the head with a stone to make sure of it, and turned to watch again. My father caught ten sharks this way, grabbing their tails and sending them arcing out over our heads to the rocks behind, with us all watching and shouting out 'Mango, Mango,' yelling and jumping about on the rocks.

The other place, Waiariki, is very special to me. Special because it carries my name which is a very old name, and belonged to my grandfather and to others before him as well. It is a gentle quiet place where the lagoons are always clear and the brown rocks stand bright and sharp against the sky. This was a good place for crayfish and agar. Mum was the one who usually went diving for crayfish, ruku koura. She would walk out into the sea fully clothed and lean down into the water, reaching into the rock holes and under the shelves of rock for the koura. Sometimes she would completely submerge, and sometimes we would see just a little bit of face where her mouth was, sitting on top of the sea.

The rest of us would feel round in the lagoons for agar. Rimurimu we called it. For the coarse agar we would need to go out to where there was some turbulence in the water, to pluck the hard strands from the rocks. But the finer rimurimu was in the still parts of the lagoons and we would feel round for it with our feet and hands, and pick it and put it into our sugar bags.

When our bags were full we would take the agar ashore and spread it on the sand to dry. Then we'd put it all into a big bale and tramp it down. We had a big frame of timber to hold the bale, and our own stencil to label it with. I don't know how much we were paid for a bale in those days. But I do remember once, after one of the cheques had arrived, my father went to town and came home in a taxi with a rocking horse and two guitars. He handed me one of the guitars and I tuned it up and strummed on it, and I remember thinking that it was the most beautiful sound I had ever heard.

And another time my father brought home a radio, and after that our neighbours and relations used to come every week to listen to *Gentleman Rider* or the *Hit Parade*. And when the boxing or wrestling was on people would come from everywhere. We'd all squeeze into our kitchen and turn the radio up as loud as it would go. On the morning after the fights we boys would go down to the beach and find thick strands of bull kelp and make our own boxing belts and organise our own boxing or wrestling tournaments on the sand.

The horses were very useful to us then. They were of more use to us than a car or truck would have been. Besides using them for excursions round the beach we used them for everyday work, and when the rain came and flooded the creek our horses were the only means we had of getting to town. All of our wood for the range was brought down from the hills by the horses too.

On the days when we were to go for firewood we boys would go up back before breakfast and bring the horses down, and after breakfast we'd prepare the horses for the day's work. Dad would sort out all the collars and chains, and we'd go out into the yard, put the collars on the horses, and hook the long coils of chain onto the hames. Then we'd get together the axes and slashers and start out down and across the creek, and go up on to the scrub covered hills about a mile from the house.

It was always the younger boy's job to trim the leaves and side branches from the felled manuka and stack the wood on to the track ready to be chained into loads for the horses to pull. One of the older boys who had been chopping would come down and wrap the short chains round the stacks, then hook the long chains from either side of the horses' collars on to each side of the load.

Once when I was about nine years old my father and mother were at the bottom of the hill stacking the wood into cords—we were selling wood then—for the trucks to come and take away to town. My older brothers were chopping and stacking at the top of the hill and my sisters and I were taking the horses down with the loads. I was on my way up the hill on Blue Pony and my sister was at the top hitching a load to Punch, who was a good willing horse but very shy. Erana accidently bumped the chain spreader against Punch's leg and away he went. I saw Punch coming, bolting towards me with the chains flying, but it was too late to do anything. Punch knocked Blue Pony down, and I went hurtling out over the bank like Dad's mango thrown out of the lagoon.

I landed in scrub and fern and wasn't hurt. Everyone came running to look at me, but I got up laughing, and I remember my father saying, 'E tama, that one flying!' Then he went off to rescue Punch who was by then caught up in one of the fences by his chains.

On warm nights we used to like to go fishing for shark from the beach. Mangoingoi. We'd go down to the beach with our lines and bait and light a big fire there, and on some nights, especially when the sea was muddy after rain and we knew the sharks would be feeding close to the shore, there would be people spread out all along the beach, and four or five fires burning and cracking in the night.

We always used crayfish for bait, and because crayfish flesh is so soft we would bind it to our hooks with light flour bag string. Then we would tie the ends of our lines to a log and prepare the remainder so that the full length of it would be used once it was thrown. We'd walk out into the sea then, twirling the end of the line with the hooks and horseshoe on it, faster and faster, then let it go. And the line would go zipping out over the sea, and sometimes by the fire's light we'd see the splash out off shore, where the horseshoe sinker entered the water.

We waited after that, sitting up on the beach with our lines tied to our wrists. We'd talk, or sometimes sleep, and after a long while, usually an hour or more, someone's line would shoot away with shark.

'Mango, Mango!'

'Aii he mango!'

And we would all tie our lines and go running to the water's edge, 'Mango, Mango,' to watch the shark being pulled in with its tail flapping and water splashing everywhere.

Mum used to cut the shark into thick pieces and boil it, then skin it. Then she'd put it into a pan to cook with onions, and we'd eat till we were groaning. Sometimes we would hang strips of shark flesh on the line to dry, and when this had dried out we would put it in the embers of our outside fire to cook. There was one teacher at school who used to get annoyed when we'd been eating dried shark at lunchtime. He'd march around the classroom flinging the windows open and saying, 'You kids have been eating shark again. You pong.' And we'd sniff around at each other wondering what all the fuss was about.

Dad used to hang the shark liver on the line too, and let the oil drip into the stomach bag. Then he'd put the oil in a bottle and save it to treat the saddles and bridles with.

I went back to the old place last summer and took my wife and children with me for a holiday. I wanted them to know the quiet. I wanted them to enjoy the peace, and to do the things we used to do.

In most ways the holiday was all I hoped it would be. My parents still live there in much the same way as before, even though the house seems somewhat empty now with only the two of them, and two grandsons living there. Most of the other families have moved away. The vegetable gardens are not as extensive now because there is not the need, but flowers and trees are as abundant as ever, and the summer house is still there with my father's ferns flourishing and the begonias blooming.

Electricity hasn't reached that far yet, so it is still necessary for the old people to bring the wood down from the hills, and I don't like to think of them doing this on their own with only two small boys to help.

My wife and children had a good holiday. We spent two days getting firewood so that there would be plenty there after we had gone. Punch, Blue Pony, Creamy, and Crawford are all dead now, and the two horses that they use are getting old too. There are other younger horses on the hills, but with no one to break them in they are completely wild.

I took my family up on the hills and we sat looking out over the sea. I told them about the whale I had once seen out past the point, and about the American fleet, all lit, going silently by.

And one night I took them down to the beach fishing. Mangoingoi. We caught a little shark too, and Mum cooked it for us in the old way and my father hung strips of it to dry and caught the oil in the stomach bag for the bridles and saddles.

Another day we all went round the beach for kai moana and, although the tides were good and the weather perfect, we were the only ones there on the beach that day. We visited all the favourite places and took something from each. And when we came to Waiariki, which even now I think of as my own special place, I told my children its name, and that it was special to me because I had that name and so had others before me. And my little boy said to me, 'Dad why can't we stay here forever?' because he has the name as well.

But when we arrived at the first place with our knives and bags and kits and dismounted from the horses, and looked out over the flat rocks of Huapapa which is the best place for kai moana, I felt an excitement in me. I wanted to reap in abundance. I wanted to fill the kits full of good food from the sea. And then, I wanted to tell my children to put their kits down on the sand and mimi on them so that we would find plenty of good kai moana to take home. I wanted to say this to them but I didn't. I didn't because I knew they would think it unclean to mimi on their kits, and I knew they would think it foolish to believe that by so doing, their kits would be more full of sea food than if they hadn't.

And when we left the rocks with our kits only half filled I felt regret deep in me. I don't mean that I thought it was because of my children not christening their kits as we stood on the beach that we were unable to fill our bags that day. There are several reasons, all of them scientific, why the shellfish beds are depleted. And for the few people living there now, there is still enough.

No. My regret came partly in the knowledge that we could not have the old days back again. We cannot have the simple things. I cannot have them for my children and we cannot have full kits any more. And there was regret in me too for the passing of innocence, for that which made me unable to say to my children, 'Put your kits on the sand little ones. Mimi on your kits and then wash them in the sea. Then we will find plenty. There will be plenty of good kai moana in the sea and your kits will be always full.'

AND SO I GO

Our son, brother, grandchild, you say you are going away
from this place you love, where you are loved. Don't go. We
warm you. We give you strength, we give you love.
These people are yours.
These hills, this soil, this wide stretch of sea.
This quiet place.

This land is mine, this sea, these people. Here I give
love and am loved but I must go, this is in me. I go to learn
new ways and to make a way for those who follow because
I love.

My elders, brothers and sisters, children of this place,
we must go on. This place we love cannot hold us always.
The world is large. Not forever can we stay here warm and
quiet to turn the soil and reap the sea and live our lives.
This I have always known. And so I go ahead for those who
come. To stand mid-stream and hold a hand to either side.
It is in me. Am I not at once dark and fair, fair and dark?
A mingling. Since our blue-eyed father held our dark-eyed
mother's hand and let her lead him here.

But, our brother, he came, and now his ways are hers out
of choice because of love.

And I go because of love. For our mother and her
people and for our father. For you and for our children
whose mingling will be greater than our own. I make a way.
Learn new ways. So I can take up that which is our father's
and hold it to the light. Then the people of our mother
may come to me and say, 'How is this?' And I will hold

the new thing to the light for them to see. Then take up that which is our mother's and say to those of our father, 'You see? See there, that is why.'

And brother, what of us. Must we do this too? Must we leave this quiet place at the edge of hills, at the edge of sea and follow you? For the sake of our mother's people who are our own. And for our father and because we love?

You must choose but if you do not feel it in you, stay here in warmth. Let me do this and do not weep for my going. I have this power in me. I am full. I ache for this.

Often I have climbed these hills and run about as free as rain. Stood on the highest place and looked down on great long waves looping on to sand. Where we played, grew strong, learned our body skills. And learned the ways of summers, storms, and tides. From where we stepped into the spreading sea to bathe or gather food. I have watched and felt this ache in me.

I have watched the people. Seen myself there with them living too. Our mother and our blue-eyed father who came here to this gentle place that gives us life and strength. Watched them work and play, laugh and cry, and love.

Seen our uncle sleeping. Brother of our mother. Under a tree bright and heavy with sunned fruit. And beside our uncle his newest baby daughter sleeping too. And his body-sweat ran down and over her head in a new baptising. I was filled with strength.

And old Granny Roka sits on her step combing her granddaughter's hair, patiently grooming. Plaiting and tying the heavy tangled kelp which is her pride. Or walk together on the mark of tide, old Granny and the child, collecting sun-white sticks for the fire. Tying the sticks into bundles and carrying them on their backs to the little house. Together.

And seen the women walk out over rocks when the tide is low, submerging by a hole of rock with clothes ballooning. Surfacing with wine-red crayfish, snapping tails and clawing

air on a still day. And on a special day the river stones
fired for cooking by our father, our cousins, and our uncles
who laugh and sing. Working all as one.

Our little brother's horse walks home with our little one
asleep. Resting a head on his pony's neck, breathing in
the warm horse stink, knees locked into its sides. Fast
asleep on the tired flesh of horse. And I ache. But not forever
this. And so I go.

And when you go our brother as you say you must will
you be warm? Will you know love? Will an old woman kiss
your face and cry warm tears because of who you are? Will
children take your hands and say your name? In your new
life our brother will you sing?

The warmth and love I take from here with me and
return for their renewal when I can. It is not a place of
loving where I go, not the same as love that we have known.

> No love fire there to warm one's self beside
> No love warmth
> Blood warmth
> Wood and tree warmth
> Skin on skin warmth
> Tear warmth
> Rain warmth
> Earth warmth
> Breath warmth
> Child warmth
> Warmth of sunned stones
> Warmth of sunned water
> Sunned sand
> Sand ripple
> Water ripple
> Ripple sky
> (Sky Earth
> Earth Sky
> And our beginning)

And you ask me shall I sing. I tell you this. The singing will be here within myself. Inside this body. Fluting through these bones. Ringing in the skies of being. Ribboning in the course of blood to soothe swelled limbs and ache bruised heart.

You say to us our brother you will sing. But will the songs within be songs of joy? Will they ring? Out in the skies of being as you say? Pipe through bone, caress flesh wounding? Or will the songs within be ones of sorrow.

> *Of warmth dreams*
> *Love dreams*
> *Of aching*
> *And flesh bruising.*
> *If you listen will it be weeping that you hear?*
> *Lament of people*
> *Earth moan*
> *Water sigh*
> *Morepork cry of death?*

My sisters, brothers, loved ones, I cannot tell. But there will be gladness for me in what I do. I ask no more. Some songs will be of joy and others hold the moan and sigh, the owl cry and throb of loneliness.

What will you do then our brother when the singing dirges through your veins, pressing and swelling in your throat and breast, pricking at your mind with its aching needles of sound?

What should I do but deny its needling and stealing into mind. Its pressing into throat and breast. I will not put a hand of comfort over body hardenings nor finger blistered veins in soothing. The wail, the lament shall not have my ear. I will pay the lonely body ache no mind. Thus I go.

I stand before my dark-eyed mother, blue-eyed father, brothers, sisters. My aunts and uncles and their children and these old ones. All the dark-eyed, light-eyed minglings of this place.

We gather. We sing and dance together for my going.

We laugh and cry. We touch. We mingle tears as blood.
I give you my farewell.

Now I stand on a tide-wet rock to farewell you sea. I listen
and hear your great heart thud. I hear you cry. Do you too
weep for me? Do you reach out with mottled hands to
touch my brow and anoint my tear-wet face with tears of
salt? Do not weep but keep them well. Your great heart
beats I know for such as these. Give them sea, your great
sea love. Hold them gently. Already they are baptised in
your name.

> As am I
> And take your renewal where I go
> And your love
> Take your strength
> And deep heart thud
> Your salt kiss
> Your caring.

Now on a crest of hill in sweeping wind. Where I have
climbed and run. And loved and walked about. With life
brimming full in me as though I could die of living.

Guardian hill you do not clutch my hand, you do not
weep. You know that I must go and give me blessing.
You guard with love this quiet place rocking at the edge
of sea . . .

And now at the highest place I stand. And feel a power
grip me. And a lung-bursting strength. A trembling in my
legs and arms. A heavy ache weighting down my groin.

And I lie on soil in all my heaviness and trembling.
Stretch out my arms on wide Earth Mother and lay my face
on hers. Then call out my love and speak my vow.

And feel release in giving to you earth, and to you sea,
to these people.

So I go. And behind me the sea-moan and earth-cry, the
sweet lament of people. Towards the goddess as she sleeps
I go. On with light upon my face.

HURIA'S ROCK

Old now these bones, and one leg with a stick to help it. old now. He sits, this old one with his stick, on the beach and the agar about him all spread to dry. It is good, the stick, to turn the spread agar, and to poke the ashes round the big camp oven.

~ She makes the camp oven bread, my daughter, in the morning early, early, as did the mother before her. Good bread, this of the camp oven, and the work of this old one to poke the ashes and turn the spread agar with the stick.

Too old now these bones and this leg for the work of young days, and so they go, those of young days to collect the agar from the sea, while this old one he tends the fire and with the stick turns the agar to dry. His work too, to guard the little one who sleeps there in the tent. A great-grandson this, who sleeps on his rug in the tent. He wakes, this young one, then it is the work of this old one to wave his stick for the mother to come and tend him. But no— sleeps the little one. Sleeps he.

Soon they will return, those who gather agar, with kits full and backs tired. Back to camp to rest and eat, then before nightfall to pick up the dried agar and tramp it into the bale. Then to get ready the beds in the tent and then to sleep, for it is much work this gathering of agar.

Many years now since last we came to camp and gather agar here. Young days then I, and the leg without a stick to help it. Two good legs then, and a back strong. Two good eyes, and the hands to pull the agar from the warm sea.

But a sad time that, when last we came to this place. Died here, my wife, when last we came. Drowned she, under crayfish rock, now named Huria's rock for her. No more to that rock since then for crayfish. We leave it to her, to Huria—it is her resting place.

It was large, the crowd that came that year for agar. A good tide that day—the day she died—and the top of crayfish rock showing above the water. Many were there gathering agar in shallow water, but Huria, she took her kit and started out to crayfish rock and took our boy with her. We who picked the agar could see the boy sitting on the rock with the kit, and many times Huria came to him with crayfish.

A good day for crayfish this, thought I. A good day and a good time.

Then looked again to the rock, and the boy he stood looking into the water. Waiting and looking, with the crayfish from the kit crawling about him on the rock.

To the rock then I, calling her name. The others, they left the agar and came behind me for they had seen the spilled crayfish, and the boy waiting and looking down into the sea.

A sad time this. Caught in a crack of the rock we found her, and much work it was to free her for we who mourned.

Lonely years since then for this old one who sits now on the beach. But she will come soon, Huria, for the old one with the stick. She will come for he who looks to her rock and thinks of her, while those of young days gather agar from the sea.

Look now, to Huria's rock thinking of Huria, and now I see her sitting there on the rock. Look away then I, for they are old now, these eyes. But then back again to the rock and still she sits. It is Huria. She has come.

'For this old one?' I call. But her head is turned away.

'Huria, Huria,' but she looks not at me.

'It is time then, for this old one?' I say.

But she moves then, Huria. Puts out her hand to the tent.

To the tent then I, quickly, with the stick working for the leg. Into the tent. But he sleeps, the little one, sleeps peacefully. Out then and looking to the rock, and still she sits Huria, still she looks to the tent.

'Sleeping, the young one,' I call. 'Come not for the young but the old.'

Then stands Huria, and moves nearer, looking to the tent.

Quickly then I, to the lagoon where they gather agar, and wave my stick. She waves, the mother of the little one, and comes to me.

'He is sick, the little one. Go to your baby,' I say.

Drops the kit of agar then, and runs to the tent.

'He sleeps, Grandpa,' she calls from the tent.

'Go to him,' I say. 'He is sick. Huria, she comes for the little one.' I show her Huria but she does not see.

'You sit too much in the sun Grandpa,' she says. 'And you think too much of Huria. It was wrong to come to this place for agar. It was bad to bring you here.'

'Huria she is close,' I say to her, and I pull her into the tent with me, to the little one.

Screams then, and pulls my stick from my hand.

'The spider Grandpa—the katipo,' and beats at the blanket where sleeps the young one. Beats and beats the katipo with the stick. Picks up the little one then as he wakes and cries.

'Safe my baby,' she says. 'Our Grandpa has saved you. Safe now,' says she.

Out then I, to look for one who gave us warning. But gone, Huria. Gone she who helped the old one guard the young.

But tired, the old one. Tired. And soon she will be back, Huria, for the old one with the stick.

Soon she comes.

VALLEY

Summer

The sun-filled sky wraps the morning in warmth. Already the asphalt has begun to shimmer with light and heat, and the children are arriving.

They spill out of the first bus with sandwiches and cordial, in twos and threes, heads together, strangely quiet. Uncertain they stand with bare feet warming on asphalt, clutching belongings, wondering. They are wondering what I will be like.

It is half past eight. I am watching from my kitchen window and see them glance this way, wondering. In a minute or two I will be ready to go over for them to look at me, but now they are moving away slowly, slapping feet on the warmed playground.

They are wondering what he will be like too. He is in his classroom already, sorting out names, chalking up reminders, and cleaning dead starlings from the grate of the chipheater in the corner. They stand back from the glass doors and stare, and he comes out with the dead birds on a shovel and gives them to a big boy to take away and bury. They all stare, and the younger ones wonder if he killed the birds, but the older ones know that starlings get trapped in the chimneys every summer and have to be cleaned out always on the first day of school.

I pick up the baby and my bag and walk across. Their eyes are on me.

'Hullo,' I say, but no one speaks, and they hurry away to the middle room, which is Tahi's, because they know her. Some of them call her Mrs Kaa because they have been told to; others call her Auntie because she is their aunt; and others call her Hey Tahi because they are little and don't know so much.

At nine he rings the bell and makes a come-here sign with his arm. They see, and know what he wants, and walk slowly to stand on the square of concrete by the staffroom steps. They stand close together, touching, and he tells them his name and mine. Then he reads their names from a list and Tahi tells each where to stand. Soon we have three groups: one for the little room which is mine, one for the middle room which is hers, and one for the big room which is his.

We find a place for the sandwiches and cordial and then they sit looking at me and not speaking, wondering what I am like.

I put the baby on a rug with his toys. I put my bag by the table, then write my name on the board to show them how it looks. And I read it for them so they will know its sound. I write baby's name as well and read it too, but they remain silent.

And when I say good morning they look at one another and at the floor, so I tell them what to say. But, although some open their mouths and show a certain willingness, no sound comes out. Some of them are new and haven't been to school before and all of them are shy.

The silence frightens me, beating strongly into the room like sun through glass.

But suddenly one of them speaks.

He jumps up and points excitedly. Necks swivel.

'Hey! You fullas' little brother, he done a mimi. Na!'

And there is little Eru with a puddle at his feet. And there we are, they and I, with a sentence hanging in the sun-filled room waiting for another to dovetail its ending.

I thank him and ask his name but his mouth is shut again. The little girl in shirt and rompers says, 'He's Samuel.'

'Mop?' Samuel asks, and means shall I get the wet mop from the broom cupboard and clean up the puddle. Which is friendly of him.

'Yes please,' I say, but again he stands confused.

Shirt and rompers shoves him towards the door. 'Go,' she says.

He mops up the water and washes the mop at the outside tap. Then he stands on the soggy mop-strings with his warmed feet, and the water squeezes out and runs in little rivers, then steams dry. Samuel wears large serge shorts belted with a man's necktie and there is one button on his shirt. His large dark eyes bulge from a wide flat face like two spuds. His head is flat too, and his hair has been clipped round in a straight line above his ears. The hair that is left sticks straight up as though he is wearing a kina.

Shirt and rompers tells me all the names and I write them on the board. Her name is Margaret.

> Samuel
> Margaret
> Kopu, Hiriwa
> Cowboy
> Lillian, Roimata
> Glen
> Wiki, Steven
> Marama, Evelyn
> Michael, Edie
> Hippy
> Stan.

We have made a poem. The last two are twins; I don't know how I'll ever tell them apart.

We find a place for everyone at the tables and a locker for each one's belongings, but although they talk in whispers and nudge one another they do not offer me any words. And when I speak to them they nod or shake their heads. Their eyes take the floor.

The play bell rings and I let them go. They eat briefly, swig at the cordial or go to the drinking taps. Then they pad across the hot asphalt to the big field where the grass is long and dry. Then they begin to run and shout through the long grass as though suddenly they have been given legs and arms, as though the voices have at that moment been put into them.

Ahead of them the grasshoppers flick up and out into the ever-heating day.

Hiriwa sits every morning at the clay table modelling clay. He is a small boy with a thin face and the fingers that press into the clay are long, and careful about what they do.

This morning he makes a cricket—female by the pointed egg-laying mechanism on its tail. He has managed the correct angles of the sets of legs, and shows the fine rasps on the hind set by lifting little specks of clay with his pencil. Soon he will tell me a story so I can write for him; then later he will show the children what he has made and read the story for them.

We collected the crickets yesterday because we are learning about insects and small animals in summer. The crickets are housed in a large jar containing damp earth and stones and a wine biscuit. The book tells me that this is the way to keep crickets, and they seem content enough to live like this as they begin their ringing in the warmth of mid-morning.

Two weeks ago we walked down past the incinerator to where nasturtiums flood a hollow of ground at the edge of bush, covering long grass and fern beginnings with round dollar leaves and orange and gold honey flowers blowing trumpets at the sky.

The first thing was to sit among the leaves and suck nectar from the flowers, which wasn't why we had come but had to be done first. And it gave us a poem for the poem book too. Roimata, who finds a secret language inside herself, gave us the poem:

> I squeeze the tail off the nasturtium flower
> And suck the honey,
> The honey runs all round inside me,
> Making me sweet
> Like sugar,
> And treacle,
> And lollies,
> And chocolate fish.
> And all the children lick my skin
> And say, 'Sweet, sweet,
> Roimata is a sweet, sweet girl.'

The next thing was to turn each flat nasturtium leaf carefully and look on the soft green underside for the pinprick sized butterfly eggs. We found them there, little ovals of yellow, like tiny turned-on light bulbs, and found the mint-green caterpillars too, chewing holes in their umbrellas.

The next thing was to put down the leaves they had picked and to begin rolling down the bank in the long grass, laughing and shouting, which wasn't why we had come but had to be done as well:

> I rolled busting down the bank
> On cold seagrass,
> And I thought I was a wave of the sea,
> But I am only a skinny girl
> With sticking out eyes,
> And two pigtails
> That my Nanny plaits every morning
> With spider fingers.

Now all the eggs have hatched, and every afternoon they pick fresh leaves for the caterpillars. Every morning we find the leaves eaten to the stems, and the table and floor littered with black droppings like scattered crumbs of burnt toast.

The caterpillars are at several stages of growth. Some are little threads of green cotton, and difficult to see, camouflaged by the leaf and its markings. Others are half grown and working at the business of growing by eating steadily all day and night. The largest ones are becoming sluggish with growth, and have gone away from food and attached themselves to the back of the room to pupate:

> The caterpillar,
> Up on the classroom wall,
> Spins a magic house around itself
> To hide from all the boys and girls.

Then yesterday on coming in from lunch we found the first of the butterflies, wing-beating the sun-filled room in convoy. We kept them for the afternoon, then let them out the window and watched them fly away:

> Butterfly out in the sun,
> Flying high by the roof,
> 'Look up there,' Kopu said.
> 'Butterfly. Na.
> The best butterfly.
> I want to be a butterfly flying.'

I said that he would tell me a story to write about his cricket. And that later he would show the children what he had made and read the story for them. But I turned and saw his arm raised and his fist clenched. His thin arm, with the small fingers curled, like a daisy stem with its flower closed after sundown. The fist came down three times on the carefully modelled insect. Head, thorax, abdomen. He looked at what he'd done and walked away.

'Why?' I asked but he had no words for me.

'That's why, he don't like it,' Samuel told me.

'That's why, his cricket is too dumb,' Kopu said.

Those two have made a bird's nest out of clay and are filling it with little round eggs, heaping the eggs up as high as they will go.

'I made a nest.'

'I made some eggs.'

I made a cricket as best I could with my careful fingers. Then my flower hand thumped three times down on the cricket. Abdomen, thorax, head. And my cricket is nothing but clay.

Autumn

Autumn bends the lights of summer and spreads evening skies with reds and golds. These colours are taken up by falling leaves which jiggle at the fingertips of small-handed winds.

Trees give off crowds of starlings which shoot the valley with scarcely a wing beat, flocking together to replace warmth stolen by diminishing sun.

Feet that were soft and supple in summer are hardening now and, although it is warm yet, cardigans and jerseys are turning up in the lost-property box. And John, our neighbour, looks into his vat one morning and sees a single sheet of milk lining the bottom. He puts his herd out and goes on holiday.

Each day we have been visiting the trees—the silver poplar, the liquid amber, and the plum, peach, and apple. And, on looking up through the branches, each day a greater patch of sky is visible. Yet, despite this preoccupation with leaves and colours and change, the greater part of what we see has not changed at all. The gum tree as ever leaves its shed bark, shed twigs, shed branches untidily on its floor, and the pohutukawa remains dull and lifeless after its December spree and has nothing new for this season.

About us are the same green paddocks where cows undulate, rosetting the grass with soft pancake plops; and further on in the valley the variegated greens of the bush begin, then give way to the black-green of distant hills.

They have all gone home. I tidy my table, which is really a dumping ground for insects in matchboxes, leftover lunches and lost property. Then I go out to look for Eru. The boys are pushing him round in the wood cart and he is grinning at the sky with his four teeth, two top and two bottom, biting against each other in ecstasy.

Tahi is in the staffroom peeling an apple. She points the knife into the dimple of apple where the stem is and works the knife carefully in a circle. A thin wisp of skin curls out from the blade. She peels slowly round and down the apple, keeping the skin paper-thin so that there is neither a speck of skin on the apple nor a speck of apple flesh left on the skin. Nor is there a ridge or a bump on the fruit when she has finished peeling. A perfect apple. Skinless. As though it has grown that way on the tree.

Then she stands the apple on a plate and slashes it down the middle with a knife as though it is nothing special and gives me half.

'Gala Day in five days' time,' she says.

'Yes,' I say. 'They'll want to practise for the races.'

'We always have a three-legged and a sack.'

Then Ed comes in and picks up the phone.

'I've got to order a whole lot of stuff for the gala. Gala in five days' time.'

We wake this morning to the scented burning of manuka and, looking out, see the bell-shaped figure of Turei Mathews outlined by the fire's light against the half-lit morning. He stands with his feet apart and his hands bunched on his spread waist, so that his elbows jut. With his small head and his short legs, he looks like a pear man in a fruit advertisement, except that he has a woman's sunhat pulled down over his ears.

Beside him Ron and Skippy Anderson are tossing branches into the flames and turning the burning sticks with shovels. We hear the snap, snap of burning tea tree and see the flames spread and diminish, spread, diminish—watch the ash-flakes spill upwards and outwards into lighting day.

Yesterday afternoon Turei, Ron, and Skippy brought the truckload of wood and the hangi stones and collected the two wire baskets from the hall. They spat on their hands, took up the shovels, and dug the hole, then threw their tools on the back of the truck and went.

Yesterday Ed and the boys put up the tents, moved tables and chairs, and set up trestles. The girls tidied the grounds, covered tables with newspaper, and wrote numbers in books for raffles.

We were worried by clouds yesterday. But now on waking we watch the day lighting clear; we pack our cakes and pickles into a carton and are ready to leave.

By eight o'clock the cars and trucks are arriving and heaving out of their doors bags of corn, kumara, potatoes, pumpkin, and hunks of meat. Women establish themselves under the gum tree with buckets of water, peelers, and vegetable knives. Turei and his helpers begin zipping their knives up and down steel in preparation for slicing into the pork. Tahi is organising the cakes and pickles and other goods for sale, Eru is riding in the wood cart, and Ed is giving out tins for raffle money. I take up my peeler and go towards the gum tree.

Roimata's grandmother is there.

'It's a good day,' she says.

'Yes,' I say. 'We are lucky.'

'I open these eyes this morning and I say to my mokopuna, "The day it is good." She flies all around tidying her room, making her bed, no trouble. Every smile she has is on her face. I look at her and I say, "We got the sun outside in the sky, and we got the sun inside dancing around." I try to do her hair for her. "Hurry, Nanny, hurry," she says. "Anyhow will do." "Anyhow? Anyhow?" I say. "Be patient, Roimata, or they all think it's Turei's dog coming to the gala."'

Opposite me Taupeke smokes a skinny fag, and every

now and again takes time off from peeling for a session of coughing. Her face is as old as the hills, but her eyes are young and birdlike and watchful. Her coughing has all the sounds of a stone quarry in full swing, and almost sends her toppling from the small primer chair on which she sits.

'Too much this,' she explains to me, pointing to her tobacco tin. 'Too much cigarette, too much cough.'

And Connie next to her says, 'Yes, Auntie. You take off into space one of these days with your cough.'

She nods. 'Old Taupeke be a sputnik then. Never mind. I take my old tin with me. No trouble.'

Hiriwa's mother is there too. She is pale and serious-looking and very young. Every now and again Hiriwa comes and stands beside her and watches her working; his small hands rest lightly on her arm, his wrist bones protude like two white marbles. I notice a white scar curving from her temple to her chin.

Tahi comes over and says, 'Right give us a spud,' then spreads her bulk on a primer chair and begins her reverent peeling. A tissue-thin paring spirals downward from her knife.

'How are you Auntie? How are you Connie? How are you Rita? Gee Elsie you want to put your peel in the hangi and throw your kumara away.'

'Never mind,' says Elsie. 'That's the quick way. Leave plenty on for the pigs.'

'Hullo Auntie, hullo ladies. How are all these potato and kumara getting on?' asks Turei. He takes off his sunhat and wipes the sweat from his neck and head.

'Never mind our potato and kumara,' Tahi says. 'What about your stones? Have you cooks got the stones hot? We don't want our pork jumping off our plates and taking off for the hills.'

'No trouble,' Turei says. 'The meal will be superb. Extra delicious.'

'Wii! Listen to him talk.'

'You got a mouthful there Turei!'

'Plenty of kai in the head, that's why,' he says.

'And plenty in the puku too. Na. Plenty of hinu there Turei.'

'Ah well. I'm going. You women slinging off at my figure I better go.'

He puts his hat on and pats his paunch. 'Hurry up with those vegies. Not too much of the yakkety-yak.' He ambles away followed by a bunch of kids and a large scruffy dog.

The sacks are empty. We have peeled the kumara and potatoes, stripped and washed the corn, and cut and skinned the pumpkin. The prepared vegetables are in buckets of water and we stand to go and wash our hands.

But suddenly we are showered with water. We are ankle deep in water and potatoes, kumara, pumpkin, and corn. Connie, who hasn't yet stood, has a red bucket upside down on her lap and she is decorated with peelings. Turei's dog is running round and round and looks as though he has been caught in a storm.

'Turei, look what your mutt did,' Tahi yells, and Turei hurries over to look, while the rest of us stand speechless. Taupeke's cigarette is hanging down her chin like an anaemic worm.

'That mutt of mine, he can't wait for hangi. He has to come and get it now. Hey you kids. Come and pick up all this. Come on you kids.'

The kids like Turei and they hang around. They enjoy watching him get the hangi ready and listening to him talk.

'They're the best stones,' he tells them. 'These old ones that have been used before. From the river these stones.'

The boys take their shirts off because Turei wears only a singlet over his big drum chest.

'How's that, Turei?' they ask, showing off their arm muscles.

'What's that?' he says.

'What you think?'

'I seen pipis in the sand bigger than that.'

'You got too much muscles, Turei.'

'Show us, Turei.'

'Better not. Might be you'll get your eyes sore.'

'Go on,' they shout.

So he puts the shovel down, and they all watch the big fist shut and the thick forearm pull up while the great pumpkin swells and shivers at the top of his arm.

'Wii na Turei! Some more, Turei.'

'You kids don't want any kai? You want full eyes and empty pukus?'

'Some more, Turei. Some more.'

But Turei is shovelling the white-hot stones into the hangi hole. 'You kids better move. Might be I'll get you on the end of this shovel and stick you all in the hole.'

He makes towards them and they scatter.

The prepared food is covered with cloths and the baskets are lowered over the stones. Steam rises as the men turn on the hose. They begin shovelling earth on to the covered food.

'Ready by twelve,' one of them says.

'Better be sweet.'

'Superb. Extra delicious.'

'Na. Listen to the cook talk.'

Over at the chopping arena the men finish setting up the blocks and get ready to stand to. The crowd moves there to watch as the names and handicaps are called. Hiriwa stands opposite his father's block watching.

Different, the father. Unsmiling. Heavy in build and mood. Blunt fingered hands gripping the slim handled axe.

Hiriwa watches for a while, then walks away.

The choppers stand to and the starter calls 'Go' and begins the count. The lowest handicapped hit into their blocks and as the count rises the other axemen join in. The morning is filled with sound as voices rise, as axes strike and wood splits. White chips fly.

By three o'clock the stalls have done their selling. The last bottle of drink has been sold, many of the smaller children are asleep in the cars and trucks, and the older ones have gone down to the big field to play. Some of the tents are down already and the remains of the hangi have been cleared away. At the chopping arena the men are wrenching off the bottom halves of the blocks from the final chop and throwing split wood and chips on to the trucks.

Turei's dog is asleep under a tree. Finally the raffles are drawn.

Joe Blow wins a bag of kumara which he gives to Ed. Ed wins a carton of cigarettes which he gives to Taupeke. And Tahi wins a live sheep, which she tries to put into the boot of her car but which finds its feet and runs out the gate and down the road, chased by all the kids and Turei's dog.

The kids come back and later the dog, but the sheep is never seen again.

> I said to Nanny,
> 'Do my hair anyhow,
> Anyhow,
> Anyhow,
> Today the gala is on.'
> But she said, 'Be patient, Roimata,
> They'll think it's Turei's dog.'

Winter

It rains.
The skies weep.
As do we.

Earth stands open to receive her and beside the opened
earth we stand to give her our farewell.
'Our Auntie, she fell down.' They stood by the glass
doors touching each other, eyes filling. Afraid.
'Our Auntie, she fell.'
And I went with them to the next room and found her
lying on the floor, Ed bending over her, and the other
children standing, frightened. Not knowing.
'Mrs Kaa, she has fallen on the floor.'
Rain.
It has rained for a fortnight, the water topped the river
banks then flowed over. The flats are flooded. Water stirred
itself into soil and formed a dark oozing mud causing bare
feet to become chapped and sore and hard.

'Like sky people crying,
Because the sun is too lazy
And won't get up,
And won't shine,
He is too lazy.
I shout and shout,

"Get up, get up you lazy,
You make the sky people cry,"
But the sun is fast asleep.'

The trees we have visited daily are bare now, clawing grey fingered at cold winds. Birds have left the trees and gone elsewhere to find shelter, and the insects that in other seasons walk the trunks and branches and hurry about root formations, have tucked themselves into split bark and wood-holes to winter over.

Birds have come closer to the buildings, crowding under ledges and spoutings. We have erected a bird table and every morning put out crumbs of bread, wheat, bacon rind, honey, apple cores, and lumps of fat. And every day the birds come in their winter feathers, pecking at crumbs, haggling over fruit, fat, and honey. Moving from table to ground to rooftop, then back to table.

On John's paddock the pied stilts have arrived, also in search of food, standing on frail red legs, their long thin beaks like straws, dipping into the swampy ground.

'Our Auntie she has fallen.'

I took them out on to the verandah where they stood back out of the rain, looking at the ground, not speaking. I went to the phone. Disbelief as I went to the phone.

An emptiness and an unbelieving.

Because they had all been singing an hour before, and she had been strumming the guitar. And now there was a half sentence printed on the board with a long chalk mark trailing, and a smashed stick of chalk on the floor beside her.

Because at morning break she'd made the tea and he'd said, 'Where's the chocolate cake?' Joking.

'I'll run one up tonight,' she'd said. 'But you'll have to chase the hens around and get me a couple of eggs. My old chooks have gone off the lay.'

'Never mind the eggs,' he'd said. 'Substitute something, like water.'

'Water?' It had put a grin on her face.

'Water?' It had brought a laugh from deep inside her and soon she'd had the little room rocking with sound, which is a way of hers.

Or was. But she lay silent on the schoolroom floor and he came out and spoke to them.

'Mrs Kaa is very sick. Soon the bus will come to take you home. Don't be frightened.' And there was nothing else he could say.

'Our Auntie, she fell down.'

Standing by the glass doors, the pot bellied heater in the corner rumbling with burning pine and the room steaming. She had laughed about my washing too, that morning. My classroom with the naps strung across it steaming in the fire's heat.

'I'm coming in for a sauna this afternoon. And a feed. I'm coming in for a feed too.'

Each morning the children have been finding a feast in the split logs that the big boys bring in for the fire. Kopu and Samuel busy themselves with safety pins, digging into the holes in the wood and finding the dormant white larvae of the huhu beetle.

'Us, we like these.'

And they hook the fat concertina grubs out on the pins and put them on the chip heater to cook.

Soon there is a bacon and roasted peanut smell in the room and the others leave what they are doing and go to look. And wait, hoping there will be enough to go round.

Like two figures in the mist they stood by the doors behind the veil of steam, rain beating behind them. Large drops hitting the asphalt, splintering and running together again.

Eyes filling.

'Mrs Kaa, she fell down.'

Gently they lower her into earth's darkness, into the deep earth. Into earth salved by the touch of sky, the benediction of tears. And sad the cries come from those dearest to her. Welling up, filling the void between earth and sky and filling the beings of those who watch and weep.

'Look what your mutt did Turei.'

'We always have a three-legged and a sack.'

'Water?' the room rocking with sound, the bright apple skinless on a plate, smashed chalk beside her on the floor.

'A sauna and a feed.'

'Our Auntie.'

'Mrs Kaa. . .'

It is right that it should rain today, that earth and sky should meet and touch, mingle. That the soil pouring into the opened ground should be newly blessed by sky, and that our tears should mingle with those of sky and then with earth that receives her.

And it is right too that threading through our final song we should hear the sound of children's voices, laughter, a bright guitar strumming.

Spring

The children know about spring.

Grass grows.

Flowers come up.

Lambs drop out.

Cows have big bags swinging.

And fat tits.

And new calves.

Trees have blossoms.

And boy calves go away to the works on the trucks and get their heads chopped off.

The remainder of the pine has been taken back to the shed, and the chips and wood scraps and ash have been cleaned away from the corner. The big boys make bonfires by the incinerator, heaping on them the winter's debris. Old leaves and sticks and strips of bark from under the pohutukawa and gum, dry brown heads of hydrangea, dead wood from plum, peach, and apple.

Pipiwharauroa has arrived.

'Time for planting,' he calls from places high in the trees.

'Take up spade and hoe, turn the soil, it's planting time.'

So we all go out and plant a memorial garden. A garden that when it matures will be full of colour and fragrance.

Children spend many of their out of school hours training and tending pets which they will parade at the pet show on auction day. They rise early each morning to feed their lambs and calves, and after school brush the animals, walk them, and feed them again.

Hippy and Stan have adopted Michael, who hangs between them like an odd looking triplet. The twins have four large eyes the colour of coal, four sets of false eye lashes and no front teeth. They are a noisy pair. Both like to talk at once and shout at each other, neither likes to listen. They send their words at each other across the top of Michael's head and land punches on one another that way too.

Bang!

'Na Hippy.'

Bang!

'Na Stan.'

Bang!

'Serve yourself right Hippy.'

Bang!

'Serve yourself right Stan.'

Bang!

'Sweet ay?'

Bang!

Sweet ay?'

Until they both cry.

Michael is the opposite in appearance, having two surprised blue eyes high on his face, and no room to put a pin head between one freckle and the next. His long skinny limbs are the colour of boiled snapper and his hair is bright pink. Without his shirt he looks as though the skin on his chest and the skin on his back is being kept apart by mini tent poles. His neck swings from side to side as Hippy punches Stan, and Stan punches Hippy. And Michael joins in the chorus. 'Na Hippy! Sweet? Sweet Stan ay? Serve yourself right.' And when they both cry he joins in that as well.

New books have come, vivid with new ink and sweet with the smell of print and glue and stiff bright paper.

We find a table on which to display the books, and where they can sit and turn the pages and read. Or where I can sit and read for them and talk about all the newly discovered ideas.

'Hundreds of cats, thousands of cats, millions and billions and trillions of cats.'

'Who goes trip trap, trip trap, trip trap over my bridge?'

'Our brother is lost and I am lost too.'

'Run, run, as fast as you can, you can't catch me I'm the gingerbread man?'

Hiriwa makes a gingerbread man with clay, and Kopu and Samuel make one too.

Out of the ovens jump the gingerbread men, outrunning the old woman, the old man, the cat, the bear. 'That's why, the gingerbread man is too fast.' Then is gone in three snaps of the fox's jaws. Snip, Snap, Snap. Which is sad they think.

'Wii, the fox.'

'Us, we don't like the fox.'

'That's why, the fox is too tough.'

'Cunning that fox.'

Then again the closed hand comes down on clay. Snip. Snap. Snap.

He writes in his diary, 'The gingerbread man is lost and I am lost too.' One side of his face is heavy with bruising.

On the day of the pet show and auction his mother says to me, 'We are going away, Hiriwa and I. We need to go, there is nothing left for us to do. By tomorrow we will be gone.' I go into the classroom to get his things together.

The cars and trucks are here again. The children give the pets a drink of water and a last brush. Then they lead the animals in the ring for the judges to look over, discuss, award prizes to. Some of the pets are well behaved and some are not. Patsy's calf has dug its toes in and refuses to budge, and Patsy looks as though she is almost ready to take Kopu's advice. Kopu is standing on the sideline yelling, 'Boot it in the puku Patsy. Boot it in the puku.' And when the judges tell him to go away he looks put out for a moment. But then he sees Samuel and they run off together, hanging on to each other's shirts calling, 'Boot it in the puku. Boot it in the puku,' until they see some-body's goat standing on the bonnet of a truck, and begin rescue operations.

Inside the building, women from W.D.F.F. are judging cakes and sweets and arrangements of flowers. I go and help Connie and the others prepare lunch.

'Pity we can't have another hangi,' Connie says.

'Too bad, no kumara and corn this time of the year,' Elsie says. 'After Christmas, no trouble.'

Joe Blow stands on a box with all the goods about him. He is a tall man with a broad face. He has a mouth like a letter box containing a few stained stumps of teeth which grow out of his gums at several angles. His large nose is round and pitted like a golf ball, and his little eyes are set deep under thick grey eyebrows which are knotted and tangled like escape proof barbed wire. Above his eyebrows is a ribbon width of corrugated brow, and his hair sits close on top of his head like a small, tight-fitting, stocking stitch beanie. His ears are hand sized and bright red.

'What am I bid ladies, gentlemen, for this lovely chocolate cake? Who'll open the bidding?
Made it myself this morning, all the best ingredients.
What do I get, do I hear twenty-five?
Twenty I've got. Thirty I've got.
Forty cents.
Forty-five.
Forty-five. Forty-five. Gone at forty-five to my old pal Charlie, stingy bugger. You'll have to do better than that mates. Put your hands in your pockets now and what do I get for the coffee cake?. Made it and iced it myself this morning. Walnuts on top. Thirty.

I have thirty. Thirty-five here.

Forty-five. Advance on forty-five come on all you cockies, take it home for afternoon tea.

Fifty I have, keep it up friends.

Fifty-five. Sixty, now you're talking.

Sixty-five, sixty-five, seventy.

Seventy again. Seventy for the third time. Sold at seventy and an extra bob for the walnuts, Skippy my boy.

Now this kit of potatoes. What am I bid?'

'Do we keep the kit?' someone calls.

'Did I hear fifty? Fifty? Fifty I've got. Any advance on Fifty?

'Do we keep the kit too?'

'Seventy-five I've got. Come on now grew them myself this morning. Make it a dollar. A dollar I've got.'

'What about the kit?'

'One dollar fifty I've got. One seventy-five. Make it two. Two we've got. Two once, two twice, two sold. Sorry about the kit darling we need it for the next lot.' He tips the potatoes into her lap and gives the kit to one of his helpers to refill.

'Two geranium plants for the garden. Two good plants. What do I get? Come on Billy Boy, take them home for the wife. Make her sweet.'

'I already got something for that.'

'That's had it man, say it with flowers.'

'I got much better.'

'Skiting bugger, twenty-five I've got. Thirty I've got. Advance on thirty? Forty. Forty. Forty again. Forty, sold!'

'Now here's one especially for Turei. Filled sponge decorated with peaches and cream. Come on cook, I'll start you off at forty.

Forty cents ladies, gents, and Charlie, from our friend Turei at the back. And forty-five at the front here, come on Turei. Sixty?

Sixty. And seventy up front.

Eighty. Ninety.

One dollar from the district's most outstanding hangi maker and a dollar twenty from the opposition.

One dollar fifty. Two? Two up front. Two fifty from the back.

Two fifty, two fifty. . . Three.

Three we have, come on friend.

Three fifty. What do you say Turei?

Five. Five from the back there.

Five once, five twice, five sold. One cream sponge to Turei the best cook in the district. Thank you boys.

Time's getting on friends. What do you say to a leg a mutton, a bunch a silver beet, a jar a pickle, a bag a spuds, there's your dinner. A dollar? Two? Two ten, twenty, fifty, seventy. Two seventy. two seventy, two seventy, no mucking around, sold.

Another kit of potatoes. I'll take them myself for fifty. Will you let me take them home for fifty? Seventy. Seventy to you, eighty to me. Ninety to you, a dollar to me. Dollar twenty, OK, one fifty. Let me have them for one fifty? One fifty to me, ladies and gents and Charlie. One seventy-five? OK, one ninety. Two?

Two we have once, two we have twice, two for the third time, sold. All yours boy, I've got two acres of my own at home.

Here we are friends, another of these lovely home made sponges. What do you say Turei. . . ?'

But Turei is away under the gum tree sharing his cake with a lot of children and his dog.

And back again to summer, with all the children talking about Christmas and holidays, their pockets bulging with ripe plums.

The branches of the pohutukawa are flagged in brilliant red, and three pairs of tuis have arrived with their odd incongrouous talking, 'See-saw, Crack, Burr, Ding. See-saw, See-saw, Ding.' By the time they have been there a week they are almost too heavy to fly, their wings beat desperately in flight in order to keep their heavy bodies airborne.

On the last day of school we wait under the pohutukawa for the bus to arrive, and a light wind sends down a shower of nectar which dries on our arms and legs and faces in small white spots.

They scramble into the bus talking and pushing, licking their skins. They heave their belongings under the seats and turn to the windows to wave. Kopu and Samuel who are last in line stand on the bus step and turn.

'Goodbye,' Kopu says, and cracks Sam in the ribs with his elbow.

'Goodbye,' Samuel says and slams his hands down on top of his kina and blushes.

As the bus pulls away we hear singing. Waving hands protrude from the windows on either side. Hippy, Michael, and Stan have their heads together at the back window, and Roimata is there too, waving, chewing a pigtail—

> 'I am a tui bird,
> Up in the pohutukawa tree,
> And a teacher and some children came out
> And stood under my tree,
> And honey rained all over them,
> But I am a tui bird,
> And when I fly
> It sounds like ripping rags.'

SMOKE RINGS

The cheque arrived this morning—forty-one cents. Forty-one, that's my money for Athletic Park. It comes at about this time every year, and when I see the brown envelope with the window, and all my long names printed on it I know what it is and I dump it straight into the rubbish bin. Forty-one cents!

I know I could've given it to the kids to take down to the shops and spend, or I could've bought myself a packet of cigarettes. But no, every year when that money arrives I chuck it out, and that's my own way of quietly protesting. Well who wants it anyway?

Even if I am broke.

I needed a smoke too, and I still do. I've been working hard all morning trying not to think about wanting a cigarette, and trying not to think about how broke I am. But smoke or not, broke or not, I can do without their money, and that's why I tossed the cheque out, envelope and all.

Well it's no wonder I'm broke. We've had George and his crowd for a fortnight, and George and them eat a lot so it's no wonder.

We got a telegram from George from down South the Friday before last; he's my brother. The telegram said, 'Meet Rangatira tomorrow morning George.'

You never know what to expect when you get a telegram from him. Last January we got a message, 'Meet plane two o'clock George.' It was one o'clock when it arrived, so we hurried out to the airport and found one of George's little kids sitting on her bag in tears because we weren't there to meet her—that's George.

Then we got another telegram about two months ago with the same message, 'Meet plane two o'clock George.' The kids and I were home on our own and Rangi was away fishing somewhere out by Mana Island in a boat. Gee, it cost me four dollars twenty for a taxi to the airport, and when I got there it was a tin of mutton birds. Twenty-two mutton birds sealed in a kerosene tin.

Ah well, one thing about my brother, he always thinks of us when the mutton birds are in season.

But when this last telegram arrived, 'Meet Rangatira tomorrow morning George,' we knew it wouldn't be mutton birds because it was the wrong time of year. We didn't think it would be one of the kids travelling all the way from Gore overland, and then from Christchurch overnight in the Rangatira—though you never know with George.

So we all went down at seven a.m., walked on to the wharf, and there they all were coming down the gangway. All of them.

I stood there and bawled when I saw George and Peka and all the kids getting down off the Rangatira. I hadn't seen my brother and his family for six years. I stood there and bawled.

We squashed them into our car, seven of them with two big suitcases and a carton, Rangi and our three, and me with our fourth all but due, trying to keep my big bulk out of everyone's way.

Then when we arrived home we had to squeeze them all into our house. We cooked up a big breakfast and sat all the kids on the stairs with their plates on their laps. George, Peka, Rangi, and I sat round the table to eat and we wagged our tongues until they were ready to drop off. That first night we stayed up all night talking, and most other nights too. It's no wonder I'm tired now they've gone.

These houses here all have inside stairs. We're all propped on the side of the hill with gorse sneaking in through our top fences as soon as our backs are turned. The ones this side of the road have living areas downstairs, and bedrooms, bathroom, and toilet upstairs. So every time you need to go to the loo you hike up the stairs, which isn't so good when you're in this condition and needing to go every half hour. But it's good here, we like it. We'll buy this place one day, later on, when we get rich.

We took them sight-seeing all round Wellington. Round the hills and all the bays. And we showed them Parliament and the fountain, the buildings, the Terrace, the Quay, the Basin, the park. And George put his head out of the window when we got to Athletic Park and yelled out, 'See that blade of grass in the middle there, that's mine.'

The kids were all proud of him for owning some of Athletic Park. But when he said that, it reminded me about the money.

'Now I know why you're so rich,' I said. 'You been saving all your cheques from your land.'

And George blew his cool. 'Forty-one bloody cents. I wouldn't use it for toilet paper. I wouldn't wipe my bum on it.'

And Peka pointed out that it wouldn't be big enough for that anyway, not with the size of George's fat bum.

And then George mentioned that, well, he'd put it up someone's one of these days and that it wouldn't be before time, and the kids were all proud of him.

Rangi's just as bad as George. If it hadn't been for Rangi I'd never have thought of throwing the cheque away in the first place, I mean who knows? But that's Rangi. Big ideas. He thinks a lot.

And now here I am scrubbing, polishing, washing, cleaning, sweating, making myself sore and tired, just so I can fill up the emptiness from having them all gone.

Ah well, my house is clean and shiny. Everything's done. Bathroom shines, washing's out, floors and windows sparkling. The whole place is like a telly advert for liquid something.

And I could sit down and put my inflated legs up if... but keep on, it's the only thing to do. Upstairs, one foot dragging after the other. Out the back door, four leaden steps to the line. All dry. Pull out, the pegs and let them drop. Usually there is some pleasure in this bringing in of bright sheets and warm dry clothes, but not today. Arms and back aching. Legs swollen. Body as heavy as a kit of pipis.

And there on the edge of vision the incinerator. Papers need burning but no matches. Two steps away...but I pull the basket behind me. Inside and start folding. Plug in the iron and spread the cloth over the table, I could lay my head on it and sleep. Sheets in one pile, towels, underwear, shirts...

Or I could leave it and...

But no, shirts, underwear, tea-towels, socks. I could...

I see my hand go out slowly, the switch goes up. Two hands now, folding the cloth in half, in half again. Then my pumped up legs take me slowly towards the door. Hand on the handle. Turn. Open. Out.

Four uphill steps, legs wobble. Change direction, two more steps and begin scratching the papers aside—Weetbix box, purex roll, plastic container, supermarket bag, ripped up beer carton, envelope. My hand takes up the envelope and I drift towards the house like the girl on telly who bites chocolate and is wafted through mists, over hills and streams dressed in a plume of...smoke. Hurry. Comb through hair, go to the loo, sandals, downstairs, out.

Stepping out the Crescent in full sail, the envelope warm in my hand and all my long names looking out through its window.

Pre-schools out on their trikes. Brrrm, brrrm, faces

clamped in concentration. Wheels spinning. Or do they stand. Still. Is the reeling, wheeling, spinning in my head.

'Where you going?'

'Shop.'

'What for?'

'Smokes.'

'Hey you kids, hey you kids, you know what. She's going to the shop. She's getting smokes.'

Why not? Rangi and his big ideas. Power poles, spiking skyward, two more poles to go. Rolling forward on pnuematic legs. So what if George, (one more pole) wouldn't, (almost there) wipe his, (there and in) bum.

Take it from the envelope and put it on the counter. That's the worst of having a husband and a brother with big ideas. The till rings.

Out again, the box fitting the palm of my hand, hot slime feel of cellophane. Drop the one cent change into a pocket and step the Crescent in reverse. George wouldn't expect...flesh and blood...for want of a fag...

'Where you going?'

'Home.'

'What for?'

'Smoke.'

'Hey you kids, hey you kids, you know what...'

Quickly home, inside and up the stairs, go to the loo, sandals off, turn the element on high and rip the cellophane open. Lean over the reddening coil and draw in, draw in. Mouth fills. Swallow. I walk into the sitting room smoke seeping from my nose and mouth. Ears...Eyes...

I lay back with my feet up, puffing and blowing, room spinning. Poof, I go; one for Rangi. Poof; one for George. Poof, poof; two for me.

Then I get up and walk about the room blowing streamers in every direction. Big ideas.

I blow a double smoke ring out of my eyeballs, my hand finds my pocket and turns the one cent over for good luck.

PARADE

Yesterday I went with Hoani, Lena, and the little ones up along the creek where the bush begins, to cut fern and flax. Back there at the quiet edge of the bush with the hills rolling skyward and the sound of the sea behind me I was glad I had come home in response to Auntie's letter. It was easy there, to put aside the heaviness of spirit which had come upon me during the week of carnival. It was soothing to follow with my eyes the spreading circles of fern patterning the hills' sides, and good to feel the coolness of flax and to realise again the quiet strength of each speared leaf. It was good to look into the open-throated flax blooms with their lit-coal colours, and to put a hand over the swollen black splitting pods with the seed heavy in them.

And I thought of how each pod would soon cast aside its heaviness and become a mere shell, warped and empty, while that which had been its own heaviness would become new life. New growth and strength.

As we carried the bundles of fern and flax that we had collected and put them into the creek to keep fresh for the morning I was able to feel that tomorrow, the final day of the carnival, would be different from the ones recently passed when realisation had come to me, resting in me like stone.

'Please come for the carnival,' Auntie's letter had said. And the letter from my little cousin Ruby: 'Please come Matewai. We haven't seen you for two years.' I had felt excitement in me at the thought of returning, being back with them. And I came for the carnival as they had asked.

It was easy this morning to feel a lightness of spirit, waking to a morning so warm and fullscented, with odours rising to the nostrils as though every morning comes from inside the earth. Rich damp smells drenched every grass blade, every seeded stalk, and every cluster of ragwort, thistle and blackberry. Steaming up through the warming rosettes of cow dung. Stealing up the stems of lupin and along the lupin arms, out on to the little spread hands of lupin leaves.

And a sweet wood smell coming from the strewn chips and wood stack by the shed. A tangle of damp stinks from the fowl-yard and orchard, and from the cold rustiness of the cow-holed swamp. Some of the earth morning smells had become trapped under the hot bodies of cows, and were being dispensed, along with the cows' own milk and saliva smells, from the swinging bellies and milk-filled udders as the animals made their way poke-legged to the milking sheds. That was what it was like this morning.

And there was a breath of sea. Somewhere—barely discernible since evening had been long forgotten and the night had been shrugged aside—somewhere the sea was casting its breath at the land. It was as though it were calling to the land, and to us as we woke and walked into the day, 'I'm here, I'm here. Don't forget about me.'

The sun fingered the ridges of hills as we pulled the flax and fern from the creek and began to decorate the truck for the parade. We worked quickly, tying and nailing the fronds and leaves into place. And when we had finished, Uncle Hirini drove the truck in under some trees where the sun could not reach it, while we went inside to change into our costumes.

Auntie had sent all the children to wash in the creek, and as I watched them from the window it was like seeing myself as I had been not very long ago. As if it were my own innocence that they cast on to the willow branches with their clothes. Light had filtered through the willow branches on to the creek's surface, spreading in small pools to the creek banks and on to the patches of watercress and shafts of reed.

The sun had put a finger on almost everything by now. It had touched our houses and the paddocks and tree tops, and stroked its silver over the sea. The beach stones were warming from the sun's touching, and black weed, thrown up by the sea, lay in heaps on the shore drying and helpless in the sun's relentless stroking.

I watched the bodies falling into water warmed from the sun's touching, and fingers, not his, squeezing at large bars of yellow soap. Fingers spreading blistery trails of suds up and over legs and arms. Bodies, heads, ears. 'Wash your taringas.' Auntie from the creek bank. Backsides, frontsides, fingers, toes. Then splashing, diving, puffing, and blowing in this pool of light. Out on to the banks, rubbing with towels, wrapping the towels around, scrambling back through the willows, across the yard where the sun caught them for a moment before they ran inside to dress. It was like seeing myself as I had been such a short time ago.

Auntie stood back on the heels of her bare feet, puffing at a cigarette, and looking at me through half shut eyes. Her round head was nodding at me, and her long hair which she had brushed out of the two thick plaits which usually circled her head fell about her shoulders, and two more hanks of hair glistened under her armpits. The skin on her shoulders and back was pale in its unaccustomed bareness, cream coloured and cool looking. And there was Granny Rita stretching lips over bare gums to smile at me.

'Very pretty dia. Very pretty dia,' she kept saying, stroking the cloak that they had put on me, her old hands aged and grey like burnt paper. The little ones admiring, staring.

Setting me apart.

And I stood before them in the precious cloak, trying to smile.

'I knew our girl would come,' Auntie was saying again. 'I knew our girl would come if we sent for her.'

We could hear the truck wheezing out in the yard, and Grandpa Hohepa who is bent and crabby was hurrying everyone along, banging his stick on the floor. 'Kia tere,' he kept on saying. 'Kia tere.'

The men helped Granny Rita and Grandpa Hohepa on to the truck and sat them where they could see, then I stepped on to the platform which had been erected for me and sat down for the journey into town. The others formed their lines along each side of the tray and sat down too.

In town, in the heat of late morning, we moved slowly with the other parade floats along the streets lined with people. Past the railway station and shops, and over bridges and crossings, singing one action song after another. Hakas and pois.

And as I watched I noted again, as I had on the other carnival days of concerts and socials, the crowd reaction. I tried not to think. Tried not to let my early morning feelings leave me. Tried not to know that there was something different and strange in the people's reaction to us. And yet I knew this was not something new and strange, but only that during my time away from here my vision and understanding had expanded. I was able now to see myself and other members of my race as others see us. And this new understanding left me as abandoned and dry as an emptied pod of flax that rattles and rattles into the wind.

Everyone was clapping and cheering for Uncle Hirini and my cousin Hoani who kept jumping from the truck to the road, patterning with their taiaha, springing on their

toes and doing the pukana, making high pipping noises
with their voices. Their tongues lolled and their eyes popped.

But it was as though my uncle and Hoani were a pair
of clowns. As though they wore frilled collars and had
paint on their noses, and kept dropping baggy pants to
display spotted underwear and sock suspenders. As though
they turned cartwheels and hit each other on the head,
while someone else banged on a tin to show everyone that
clowns have tin heads.

And the people's reaction to the rest of us? The singing,
the pois? I could see enjoyment on the upturned faces and
yet it occurred to me again and again that many people
enjoyed zoos. That's how I felt. Animals in cages to be
stared at. This one with stripes, this one with spots—or a
trunk, or bad breath, the remains of a third eye. Talking,
swinging by the tail, walking in circles, laughing, crying,
having babies.

Or museums. Stuffed birds, rows of shells under glass,
the wing span of an albatross, preserved bodies, shrunken
heads. Empty gourds, and meeting houses where no one
met any more.

I kept thinking and trying not to think, 'Is that what
we are to them?' Museum pieces, curios, antiques, shells
under glass. A travelling circus, a floating zoo. People
clapping and cheering to show that they know about such
things.

The sun was hot. Auntie at the end of the row was beam-
ing, shining, as though she were the sun. A happy sun,
smiling and singing to fill the whole world with song. And
with her were all the little sunlets singing too, and stamping.
Arms out, fingers to the heart, fists clenched, hands open,
head to one side, face the front. Piupius swinging, making
their own music, pois bobbing. And voices calling the
names of the canoes—Tainui, Takitimu, Kurahaupo, Te
Arawa...the little ones in the front bursting with the full-
ness of their own high voices and their dancing hands and

stamping feet, unaware that the crowd had put us under glass and that our uncle and cousin with their rolling eyes and prancing feet wore frilled collars and size nineteen shoes and had had pointed hats clapped down upon their heads.

Suddenly I felt a need to reach out to my auntie and uncle, to Hoani and the little ones, to old Rita and Hohepa.

We entered the sports ground, and when the truck stopped the little ones scrambled down and ran off to look for their mates from school. Auntie and Hoani helped Granny Rita and Grandpa Hohepa down. I felt older than any of them.

And it was hot. The sun threw down his spinnings of heat and weavings of light on to the cracked summer earth as we walked towards the pavilion.

'Do you ever feel as though you're in a circus?' I said to Hoani who is the same age as I am. He flipped onto his hands and walked the rest of the way upside down. I had a feeling Hoani knew what I was talking about.

Tea. Tea and curling sandwiches. Slabs of crumbling fruit cake, bottles of blood-warm fizz, and someone saying, 'What're you doing in that outfit?' Boys from cousin Lena's school.

'Didn't you see us on the truck?' Lena was saying.

'Yeh, we saw.' One of the boys had Lena's poi and was swinging it round and round and making aeroplane noises.

Mr Goodwin, town councillor, town butcher, touching Uncle Hirini's shoulder and saying, 'Great, great,' to show what a great person he himself was, being one of the carnival organisers and having lived in the township all his life amongst dangling sausages, crescents of black pudding, leg roasts, rib roasts, flannelled tripe, silverside, rolled beef, cutlets, dripping. 'Great.' He was Great. You could tell by the prime steak hand on Uncle's shoulder.

Uncle Hirini believed the hand. Everyone who saw the

hand believed it too, or so it seemed to me. They were all believers on days such as these.

And the woman president of the C.W.I. shouting at Granny Rita as though Granny were deaf or simple. Granny Rita nodding her head, waiting for the woman to go away so she could eat her cake.

It was stuffy and hot in the hall with the stale beer and smoke smell clinging to its walls and floor, and to the old chipped forms and sagging trestle tables. Bird dirt, spider webs, mice droppings. The little ones had had enough to eat and were running up and down with their mates from school, their piupius swinging and clacking about their legs. Auntie rounding them all up and whispering to go outside. Auntie on her best behaviour wishing those kids would get out and stop shaming her. Wanting to yell, 'Get out you kids. Get outside and play. You spoil those piupius and I'll whack your bums.' Auntie sipping tea and nibbling at a sandwich.

We began to collect the dishes. Squashed raisins, tea dregs. The men were stacking the trestles and shifting forms. Mrs President put her hands into the soapy water and smiled at the ceiling, smiled to show what sort of day it was. 'Many hands make light work,' she sang out. We reached for towels, we reached for wet plates to prove how right she was.

Outside, people were buying and selling, guessing weights and stepping chains, but I went to where Granny Rita and Grandpa Hohepa were sitting in the shade of a tree, guarding the cloak between them.

More entertainment. The lines were forming again but I sat down by old Rita and Hohepa out of the sun's heat.

'Go,' Granny Rita was saying to me. 'Take your place.'

'I think I'll watch this time, Nanny.'

'You're very sad today, dia. Very sad.'

Granny Rita's eyes pricking at my skin. Old Hohepa's too.

'It's hot Nanny.'

A crowd had gathered to watch the group and the singing had begun, but those two put their eyes on me, waiting for me to speak.

'They think that's all we're good for,' I said. 'A laugh and that's all. Amusement. In any other week of the year we don't exist. Once a year we're taken out and put on show, like relics.'

And silence.

Silence with people laughing and talking.

Silence with the singing lifting skyward, and children playing.

Silence. Waiting for them to say something to me. Wondering what they would say.

'You grow older, you understand more,' Granny Rita said to me.

Silence and waiting.

'No one can take your eyes from you,' she said. Which is true.

Then old Hohepa, who is bent and sometimes crabby said, 'It is your job, this. To show others who we are.'

And I sat there with them for a long time. Quiet. Realising what had been put upon me. Then I went towards the group and took my place, and began to stamp my feet on to the cracked earth, and to lift my voice to the sun who holds the earth's strength within himself.

And gradually the sun withdrew his touch and the grounds began to empty, leaving a flutter of paper, trampled heads of dandelion and clover, and insects finding a way into the sticky sweet necks of empty bottles.

The truck had been in the sun all afternoon. The withered curling fern and drooping flax gave it the appearance of a scaly monster, asleep and forgotten, left in a corner to die. I helped Granny Rita into the cab beside Grandpa Hohepa.

'This old bum gets too sore on those hard boards. This old bum wants a soft chair for going home. Ah lovely dia.

Move your fat bum ova Hepa.' The old parched hand on my cheek. 'Not to worry dia, not to worry.'

And on the back of the truck we all moved close together against the small chill that evening had brought in. Through the town's centre then along the blackening roads. On into the night until the road ended. Opening gates, closing them. Crossing the dark paddocks with the hills dense on one hand, the black patch of sea on the other. And the only visible thing the narrow rind of foam curling shoreward under a sky emptied of light. Listening, I could hear the shuffle of water on stone, and rising above this were the groans and sighs of a derelict monster with his scales withered and dropping, making his short-sighted way through prickles and fern, over cow pats and stinging nettle, along fence lines, past the lupin bushes, their fingers crimped against the withdrawal of the day.

I took in a big breath, filling my lungs with sea and air and land and people. And with past and present and future, and felt a new strength course through me. I lifted my voice to sing and heard and felt the others join with me. Singing loudly into the darkest of nights. Calling on the strength of the people. Calling them to paddle the canoes and to paddle on and on. To haul the canoes down and paddle. On and on—

> 'Hoea ra nga waka
> E te iwi e,
> Hoea hoea ra,
> Aotea, Tainui, Kurahaupo,
> Hoea hoea ra.
>
> Toia mai nga waka
> E te iwi e,
> Hoea hoea ra,
> Mataatua, Te Arawa,
> Takitimu, Tokomaru,
> Hoea hoea ra.'

GLOSSARY

Ana	There
Aue	Alas
E hika! He aha te moemoea?	Hey! What's the dream?
E ta! or E tama!	Man!
E ta, ko haunga to tuna	Man, your eel stinks
E tama, he tuna	An eel, man
E tama. Kei whea to moemoea?	Man. What's happened to your dream?
Haka	Dance.
Hangi	Earth oven, or contents of earth oven
Haunga	Stinking
He aha te tai	What (time) is the tide
Hinaki	Eel trap
Hinu	Fat
Hoha	Wearisome
Huhu	Beetle, found in decaying timber
Ka hinga ta tatau crate	There goes our crate (of beer)
Kai	Food
Kai moana	Sea food
Kamakama	Full of spirits
Ka makere to tarau	Your pants will come down
Ka nui te kaita	Great in size
Kanukanu	Ragged
Ka pai ne	Good isn't it
Katipo	A type of poisonous spider
Kei whea?	Where is it?
Kia kaha	Be strong
Kia tere	Be quick
Kina	Sea egg
Ko tera taku	I'll say
Kuia	Old lady
Kumara	Sweet potato
Mango	Shark
Mangoingoi	Fish with a line from the shore
Marae	Area in front of a meeting house where official proceedings take place
Mimi	Urinate
Mo aku tamariki	For my children

Mokopuna	Grandchildren
Na!	Drawing attention to
Na! Ka puta mai te piro	Now the rot comes out
Ne?	Isn't that so?
Pai	Good
Parengo	Sea lettuce
Patua	Kill it
Paua	A shellfish
Pipi	A shellfish
Pipiwharauroa	Shining cuckoo
Piupiu	Flax skirt
Pohutukawa	A native tree
Poi	Dance in which a light ball on a string is used
Puha	Sow thistle
Pukana	Stare wildly
Puku	Stomach
Pupu	Edible sea snail
Ruku koura	Diving for crayfish
Tahae	Thief, or to steal
Taiaha	A long weapon of hard wood
Taringa	Ear
Taurekareka	Scoundrel
Teka	False
Tui	Native bird